Florence M Gerald

Adenheim and Other Poems

Florence M Gerald

Adenheim and Other Poems

ISBN/EAN: 9783337380175

Printed in Europe, USA, Canada, Australia, Japan

Cover: Foto ©Andreas Hilbeck / pixelio.de

More available books at **www.hansebooks.com**

ADENHEIM

AND

OTHER POEMS.

BY

FLORENCE M. GERALD.

ST. LOUIS:
G. I. JONES AND COMPANY.
1880.

TO

MY FATHER AND MOTHER

THIS VOLUME

IS LOVINGLY DEDICATED.

CONTENTS.

ADENHEIM.

In the courts of heaven the angels stood,
   Stringing their harps of gold;
The music arose, like odorous streams
   From a carvèd censer's mould;

In odorous streams of incense sweet,
   To the throne of the Lord Most High;
It pierced the veil, and sobbing died,
   Yet hardly would seem to die;

For it rose again, like the breath of prayer,
   And rolled in surges grand,
Till its musical echoes touched the souls
   Of men in the far earth land,

Who reverent listened, and low-voiced said,
   "The music is not of earth;
It is far too sweet for our sorrowing days,
   Too sad for our hours of mirth!"

But nathless, a great soul sometimes heard
   And held in his heart the strain,
Striving to echo again its tones,
   Oft striving, alas! in vain!

But ever the angels touched the harps,
   And ever the music rose;
Sometimes like the breath of the whirlwind strong,
   And then like the brook that flows,

Tinkling and gurgling its path along,
  Over a pebbly floor,
Till it rushes, at last, in a still blue lake,
  With a miniature cataract's roar.

But as ever the rich strains ringing rolled,
  As they touched their harps at even,
There was one that was sweeter than all the rest
  Of the thousand harps in heaven.

E'en as a garden, filled with flowers,
  Holdeth one bloom fairer far,
E'en as the sky, with million lights,
  Holdeth one brighter star

Than all the others, tho' others be sweet,
  Tho' others be silvery bright;
As the sweetest bloom of all the flowers,
  As the brightest star by night,

Was this angel one in the courts of heaven,
  Was his harp in the heavenly choir!
For the spirit of love burnt in his song
  In a strong, immortal fire!

As his sweet strains rose to the veilèd throne,
  A Voice from the shadows came;
It ran thro' the white-robed angel's form
  Like a sweet, hot breath of flame.

"Seralim" (for this was his angel name),
  "Seralim, with love so strong,
Ask a gift and I will grant it, my child,
  For the love that burns in thy song!"

Then the pure-eyed angels in heaven's choir,
    Each brow wore a golden crown,
Bent each at the voice of the Living God,
    In reverent obeisance down.

Seralim answered : " If sweeter my harp
    Than those of my brothers, Lord,
It is that Thy glory, and wisdom, and power,
    Dwell in each glowing chord.

" Yet there is one wish that lives in my heart,
    And, Father, since thou hast given
The boon to me, I would leave awhile
    My home in the courts of heaven

" For that strange, sad place, called Purgatory ;
    As far from the gates of Hell,
As it is from the gardens of Paradise,
    Where many poor souls dwell,

" Who have sinned, oh Father, but love Thee still,
    Tho' just is their punishment.
Oh ! may I fly for awhile to them ?
    An angel, from heaven sent,

" Would make their prison seem less sad ;
    I'd solace each suffering heart
With the hymns of the harp I touch for thee ;
    No more would their sad tears start ! "

And the Voice made answer unto his prayer,
    " Oh ! gentlest angel in Paradise,
Thy wish is granted ; go sing to them
    And soothe them with symphonies !

" For it seemeth good to Him, who ne'er
    Chasteneth but from love;
Thou hast thy will! go sing to them,
    Of the life that lives above ! "

Over the face of Seralim went
    A loving and tender look;
He touched his harp with a quivering hand,
    And the forms of the angels shook,

With all the reverent song of love
    That rose from the sweet-tongued strings;
His bright hair fell in a halo o'er
    The sweep of his snow-white wings;

He raised himself from his azure throne,
    He threw back his curls of gold,
He swept the harp with a master hand,
    And upward the music rolled

To the Veilèd One, in a song of praise,
    Far sweeter than e'er had been
His sweetest songs; and the angels joined
    In the chords of a deep amen!

Then spreading his rainbow wings, he flew
    To that orb, where the sorrowing souls
Shriek ever, till torture has purified
    Each stain from their earthly moulds, —

To that orb which is placed 'twixt heaven and hell,
    That echoes with groans and cries
Of souls by torturing made more pure
    For their rest in Paradise !

Unhappy ones! They see afar
   The fair courts built of pearl,
The high, white battlements above
   The sorrows of their world!

They see the glorious beings who
   Walk thro' those bright courts ever;
They see them drink from fountains fresh,
   From that immortal river,

Which flows, with crystal waters, round
   The mansions of the blest;
They see the children, white and pure,
   Unto Christ's bosom pressed!

They see the angels touch their harps,
   But ah! they cannot hear
The music, rising like a flame;
   That were to come too near

The joys of all the saints of heaven,
   Whose happiness hath no morrow!
With burning eyes they look and long
   To burst their bonds of sorrow,

And rise on wings and fly afar,
   As strong souls purified,
Until they reach the courts of heaven,
   And rest there by His side!

Sad, sorrowing ones! they lift their eyes,
   Bedimmed with hot tears' rain,
To all those glories, which they hope
   By tortured years to gain!

This thought consoles amidst their pain, —
　The hope of happier days!
It is for this the shrieking wretch
　Amidst his torture prays!

Seralim reached that grief-bound star,
　And, entering the crystal gate,
He sate him down on a blasted rock,
　That, grim as a statued fate,

Rose from the midst of the tortured ones;
　Then, folding his weary wings,
And holding his golden harp of heaven,
　His fingers swept o'er the strings;

Over the strings, and a harmony,
　That he played in the courts above,
Rose from the chords in a strain divine,
　Instinct with the spirit of love!

Rose like the note of the Paradise bird,
　Rose like an organ's roll,
Rose like a song that sprung to birth
　In the depths of an angel's soul.

Oh! the music-tones that the angel's hand
　Called from the heart of the lyre!
Oh! the love that illumined his glowing eyes!
　Oh! the love of his heart of fire!

Sweet peace fell over the wretched ones;
　No more did the victims wail,
Nor the demons torture the sorrowing souls,
　Who, with faces haggard and pale,

And great eyes burning, had suffering lived
  Thro' their doom-appointed years;
Washing away their earth-born sins
  With the floods of their salty tears!

Yes peace, sweet peace, fell o'er them all;
  Hushed were their pain-wrung cries,
Hushed were their wailings, shrieks and groans,—
  The sound of their long-drawn sighs!

As sleep to the mourner upon the earth,
  So was the angel's song
To the souls that o'er that tortured realm
  In countless millions throng.

As sleep to the mourner, as dreams to him
  Whose waking is void of hope,
As rest to the weary, as light to those
  Who deep in the darkness grope!

E'en sweeter than sleep, more restful than rest,
  More dreamy than ever a dream,
More than light after gloom, did the angel's song
To the souls of the wretched seem.

And yet *one* voice midst the stillness rose,
  One voice the song could not lull;
Ever there came a despairing cry
  From a maiden most beautiful!

" Mourn not for the lost, my lover,—
  My Adenheim, brave and true!
Mourn not for the lost, my lover,
  Tho' she mourns, alas! for you!"

Then the angel struck his harp again,
   Chord after chord would rise,
The very sweetest his deft hands knew,
   In heavenly melodies!

But still that lone voice rose aloft,
   Unheeding the angel's lyre,
Unconscious of e'en the sweetest harp
   E'er touched in the heavenly choir.

And ever she cried with a sharp, wild cry,
   Like a soul that is tempest-tossed,
"Oh Adenheim, Adenheim, brave and true,
   Mourn not, beloved, for the lost!"

The angel followed the wailing voice,
   And, chained to a gloomy rock,
He saw the spirit of a fair young girl!
   The demons stood by to mock!

He spoke to them, in his flute-like tones,
   "Does the song lull ye to rest?
And yet the maiden cries evermore,
   What sorrows oppress her breast?"

And the demons, standing idly by,
   Their torturings given o'er,
Gave answer, " Her care for another,
   Deep in her heart love's core,

" Is bitterer than all the tortures,
   The torments that we know ;
Therefore are our scorpions idle, —
   We leave her to her woe!"

Still nearer came the angel,
 Where the spirit maiden lay,
Chained to a rock adamantine,
 For many a weary day.

He spoke, and tho' the music
 Stilled not her wailing cry,
It ceased when his low voice reached her,
 With its current of sympathy.

"Oh! daughter of earth, that wailest
 Ever that same sad wail,
Tell me, my child, thy sorrows, —
 What is thy sinful tale?

" Even thy guiltiest mates
 Are stilled by the harp's sweet song;
What dark deed dost thou cry for, —
 What was thy soul's sad wrong?

" Why should the harp that soothes them
 Fail, in its melody,
To solace the torments of evil,
 That hang, like a cloud, o'er thee?"

"Oh! angel, that comest from heaven,"
 Answered the spirit one,
" Behold me suffering, chainèd
 Down to this bed of stone.

" Thou speakest to one, oh angel!
 Who, but three months ago,
Lived as a mortal of earth,
 Nor dreamed of this realm of woe, —

" Lived on that earth, and loved
    A creature of earthly sod,
More than ever, God knows,
    She loved the name of her God!

" Loved, — aye worshipped, adored him!
    Only a creature of clay;
But I turned from the spirit Eternal,
    To my heart's own idol, to pray!

" To my heart's own idol, my lover —
    Oh! Death, so cruel, so strong,
How could you tear me from him?
    Oh! how I hopelessly long

" But for one look from his eyes,
    But for one hand to hand touch;
He is weeping and mourning, I know, —
    One moment would comfort so much!

" One moment! Oh demons, your torture
    Is naught to the sharp, gnawing grief
Of my heart, at thought of his sorrow.
    Bring your torments! oh, sweetest relief!

" Bring scorpions to rouse and to sting me,
    Bring thongs to scourge me again,
Heat the links of the chains that bind me,
    Devise me some horrible pain!

" Any suffering, whate'er it may be,
    Ne'er have I felt it as yet!
Bring torments and horrors and tortures,
    And teach me but this — to forget!

" Forget!   Oh! lash of remembrance,
    I count all the days by thy stings,
  And the thought that he mourns for me ever,
    More horrible suffering brings

" Than the wails, the shrieks of the wretched,
    Than the torments, the pains I endure.
  That thought! 'twould make hell out of heaven,
    Did I live in that land of the Pure ! "

She struggled, stretched upward her white arms,
    Impalpable forms of the mist,
  As if even then she beheld him,
    Lover-like, come to the tryst.

But the strong chains that linked her and bound her
    Held her clasped to the demon of stone ;
  She struggled, but struggled all vainly,
    And fell, with a heart-piercing moan,

Down on the sad-colored rock,
    Her hands, on her white bosom, crossed,
  And cried, mid the gloom and the silence,
    " Mourn not, beloved, for the lost ! "

" How know'st thou, maiden, he mourns thee ? "
    Gently, the angel's tone
  Rose, like a prayer to the Father ;
    (He heard it upon His throne).

" Because," — and her face grew brighter,
    Even a demon could see
  How great was the love of this woman, —
    " I know with what agony

I'd have mourned for *him*, sweet angel."
   She measured his grief by what
Would have been her own had *she* sorrowed.
   Alas! that such measure is not

Always the heart's truest trial!
   We count other's tears by our own,
Nor reckon that well-springs of grief
   Flourish not in fountains of stone!

We grieve, and deep in the spirit
   Build up to *one* memory a shrine;
Bring love-flowers, lay them upon it,
   Pour o'er it remembrance's wine;

Guard it round with the towers of silence;
   Treasure there one hour of bliss,
Some letters, tear-stained and time-clouded,
   A touch, a look, and a kiss;

And fancy — oh fools! — that our idol
   Remembereth thus, far away!
Oh God! when that memory's measured
   By an hour!   Mayhap, even a day!

We fancy — blind, blind in the noon-day! —
   That even as we mourn for *him*,
He for us; but when we see plainly,
   When we sit with eyes tear-filled and dim,

And learn — oh, bitterest of sorrow! —
   Not to weigh other's grief by our own,
'Tis then that we wish, quivering mourners,
   That our hearts were but carved out of stone!

"'Twas thus that I would have mourned him."
   Oh, woman-love, strong and divine!
Who layest thy heart, as oblation,
   Upon thy divinity's shrine!

The angel-one, holy Seralim,
   Was touched by those words so tender;
He shadowed her o'er with his snowy wings,
   As if from all pain to defend her.

For the nature of angels is full of love;
   It dwelleth, perfection given,
From the hand of the One who is love Himself,
   In the souls of the sons of heaven.

His sweet voice grew sweeter than e'er before,
   With pitying tones divine,
It thrilled her suffering, bleeding heart;
   " No sorrow is like to thine ;

" Thou sufferest not for thyself alone,
   Unselfish and loving and true!
Can I minister aught to the pain of thy heart,
   How soothe it?   Aye, what may I do ? "

From the gloomy rock, with the demons round,
   Rose the form of the spirit-maid ;
She looked like a wraith of gray-white mist,
   Or clouds that the sun-rays fade, —

A wraith of the mist, of the mist was her robe,
   Of the mist was her shadowy frame,
And like to a lamp, that is half-way veiled,
   Her soul rose up in a flame!

And upward she raised her shadowy arms,
   Lifted upward her grief-hollowed eyes;
A tremor of transport ran thro' her slight form,
   As one, who with winged hope flies

In spirit again, to a loved one afar,
   Who standeth with arms open wide,
To press to his heart, in a heart-strong caress; —
   All trembling, entreating, she cried,

"Oh! give me, but give me, return to the earth
   One hour, — I crave but one hour!
One hour to soothe and to comfort his heart.
   Oh! angel, thy heavenly power

"Would not bid thee deny to this twice-tortured soul
   Such a boon! oh, happiest dower!
Tho' years in your heaven were even my own,
   I'd give them for one little hour,

"In which I might comfort my Adenheim's heart,
   Concealing all grief of my own,
And know myself blest, consolation to give,
   That for me no more may he moan!"

She ceased, with a sob and a tear in her voice;
   Her white arms imploringly still
Stretched out to the angel, his eyes turned away, —
   For angels may weep if they will,

But never in sight of another must fall
   The drops that to pity are given;
When they weep o'er our sorrows, their very tears
     turn
   To pearls, in the treasures of heaven!

"And know'st thou, maiden, what boon thou
      wouldst ask?
    Alas! I could grant it to thee!
  But that one hour over — a thousand years more
    As penalty added would be.

"If thou leavest these realms
    To return to the earth,
Tho' but for *one* moment,
    That moment were worth

"A thousand years' torture,
    A thousand years' pain!
All this must you suffer
    If you see him again.

"A thousand years, — pause, ere repeating that
    wish, —
    A thousand years added at once to thy doom!
The torments of demons, the scorpion's sting,
    If thou breakest one moment the bonds of the
      tomb."

"Oh! Spirit celestial! I'll suffer them thrice!
    I willingly brave all the tortures you tell;
If I may but see him, console him an hour,
    Then welcome, thrice welcome, the horrors of
      hell!

"You love not in heaven, or well would you know,
    One hour of comfort, to those that we love,
Is worth all the torments we suffer below,
    Is worth all the joys that await us above.

" Let me visit him, angel, I pray, for one hour,
    Then back will my spirit return,
Contented to know that I've comforted him,
    Tho' serpents and scorpions burn

" Thro' ages and ages; tho' chains bind me down,
    Tho' they scourge me with thong and with rod;
I will smile at it all, and look thro' it all
    To the merciful love of my God!"

He listened, this angel, with loving heart;
    He raised his eyes on high,
Where He was throned; he felt the rays
    From that All-seeing Eye.

He heard a voice no other heard,
    He saw what none discerned;
It bade him give the boon she craved
    Unto the soul that yearned

To see her lover.   He looked again,
    He saw the maiden stand,
With parted lip, heart-hungry eye,
    And shadowy, pleading hand.

Sweet pity whispered, " Grant her wish;
    Let the sorrowful maiden go!"
He touched her chains with a loving hand,
    And e'en as he touched them, lo!

They fell from her limbs, with a clanking crash,
    On the huge black bed of stone.
The demons watched, with fiery eyes,
    Murmuring, " Our prey is gone."

On the silence rose the angel's voice;
   He spoke, and the iron bar
That guardeth the gates of Purgatory, —
   The gates of that far-off star, —

Fell, and the tortured soul arose
   And floated away like mist,
That resting upon the mountain's top,
   Is by the sun-rays kissed.

A smile divine was on her brow
   And hovered upon her lip;
And the snowy wings that the angel gave,
   Like the sails of a white-winged ship,

Bore her away from the tortured ones,
   Till the form of mist was lost
In the deep blue gulf that lay beyond;
   'Twas the gulf that her soul had crossed

Three months ago. It seemed so long
   Since into those depths she was hurled.
One moment more and the maiden's soul
   Entered the human world!

*　　*　　*　　*　　*　　*　　*　　*

'Twas night, and in the castle's halls
   The minstrel sang his story;
Without, on many a battlement
   The snow lay white and hoary.

Without was winter's icy touch,
   Like glass the rivers lay;
Since they buried fair Ida beneath the earth,
   Three months had passed away.

2

Without were the leafless, gaunt-limbed pines,
  Without was the wintry breeze,
That sighed around the turrets tall, —
  Within was a scene of ease.

'Twas the banquet night, and the oaken halls
  Rang with the sounds of mirth;
The minstrel, touching his well-loved harp,
  Sang of his lord's high birth;

Sang of his deeds, well-known to fame,
  Sang of his fathers old,
And the lord's cheek flushed with pride's dark
      flame,
  Oh, handsome was he, and bold!

He sat at the head of the glittering board;
  Around him, the courtiers grand,
Laughed loud and long, as the jest went round, —
  In truth, 'twas a merry band!

And one laughed louder than all the rest,
  With a voice like a sweet bell's chime;
That one was the lord of the banquet board,
  The young lord, Adenheim!

He quaffed the wine from the goblet's brim,
  All crusted with leaves of gold,
And drank a toast to his lady fair,
  "To the love that ne'er grows cold!"

At his own right hand, on a velvet couch,
  She lay, as fair as a dream.
On her raven hair was a wreath of pearls,
  And a blush on her cheek of cream;

The splendorous gloom of her great dark eyes
    Flashed out and entranced the soul.
Lord Adenheim gazed on her face again,
    Then, raising the jewelled bowl, —

" Bitter are winds without us,
    Colder the sharp winds blow ;
Woe to the soul who travels
    To-night, 'mid the drifts of snow !

" But why should I sing of these,
    When safe in the castle walls
We are eating and making merry ;
    Echo the oaken halls !

" Let us join together, my comrades,
    In the words of a sweet wine-song ;
Drink to the maid that is fairest,
    Drink to the love that is long,

" Drink to the queen of the banquet,
    Drink to the queen of my soul !
The lady, whose love is sweeter
    Than the wine in the frosted bowl ! "

They raised on high each crystal cup,
    Brimming o'er with amber wine,
And drank to the lady of Falconberg,
    The beauty of all the Rhine !

Still louder and louder the laugh went round,
    Still merrier the jest was told.
Lord Adenheim bent and whispered low,
    " My lady, why now so cold ? "

He whispered low, in her sea-shell ear,
   Full many a love-vow sweet.
The crimson flush on her fair cheek came,
   And quicker her heart's blood beat;

But she laughed, as she shook her dark curls back,
   " Lord Adenheim, now, for shame !
You whispered to Ida, the maid who died,
   These love-words all the same !

" How can I think that your vows are true,
   When, but three months ago,
You swore that your heart would ne'er forget
   That one beneath the snow.

" Three little months since the maiden died,
   And yet you have forgot !
To your oaths and vows short shrift you've given ;
   Short 'membrance this, God wot ! "

" By my halidom," quoth the laughing lord,
   " By my halidom, lady fair,
You do me wrong with thoughts like these !
   No other lips would dare

" To breathe the words that thou hast said,
   To mock thy beauty so.
What ! I love Ida ?   Worship her,
   And whisper love-words low

" And passionate, as those I breathe
   Upon thy beauty's shrine ?
Nay, mock me not !   Injustice 'tis
   To both my love and thine !

" Compared with thee, her pale face seems
    As moon beside the sun ;
Her eyes were dull beside thy orbs,
    My proud and beauteous one !

" A few gay words I gave to her, —
    A jest, a laugh, a smile ;
A few light-wingèd, merry hours,
    I spent with her erst while.

" This all the love I gave to her, —
    The courtesy of the hour,
A song wherein I praised her face,
    A music-gift or flower.

" And was it fault, fair one, of mine,
    That she, poor fool, construed
To vows of love the courtesies
    Of one, who is not rude ?

" No fault of mine, sweet Falconberg !
    But *one* I care to woo.
She loved me ! Tush ! But all my heart
    Is virgin pure for you !"

" Nay," said the lady, " but you grieved
    For Ida's early loss ;
I mind me now, how once you knelt
    Beside the carvèd cross

That marks her grave, now wrapped in snow,
    And wept with broken heart,
And cried aloud, ' Oh ! cruel death !
    Why are we forced to part !'"

" Yea, verily, I wept awhile, —
　　A week, it was no more!
But in thine eyes a balm I found, —
　　'Twould soothe a heart more sore

" Than ever mine o'er Ida's loss.
　　I swear, I loved her not!
Steeped in the charms of thy bright face,
　　The world is all forgot!

" I love but one, imperial maid!
　　Of one fair face I dream;
That heart, sweet one, is not so cold
　　As you would have me deem.

" Thine eyes do answer back my love,
　　Thy olive cheek is flushed
With crimson tide, like scarlet wine
　　From purple clusters crushed.

" Thy voice is low; so whisper, sweet,
　　One love-word in mine ear!
That one love-word, if possible,
　　Will make thee still more dear! "

His strong right arm encirclèd
　　Her slender, girdled waist;
Low, lover-like, he bent his head
　　Her honeyed lips to taste.

But as he bent that face above,
　　A deep sigh sadly rose;
He, startled, turned and saw a sight
　　That all his warm blood froze!

A misty form! one glimpse he caught,
   Then slow it faded 'way.
She knew enough! what need was there
   One moment more to stay?

He needed not her comforting,
   And why should she reveal,
In living form, the spirit which
   Had broken thro' death's seal,

To find, — oh! tortured, faithful heart, —
   To find man's love was not
A thing of heaven, but earthly bloom, —
   To find she was forgot!

But three short months! The drifts of snow,
   That wrapped her earthly bed,
Were not more cold than his false heart;
   Thus do we shrine our dead!

   *   *   *   *   *   *   *   *

" So soon returned," the angel said,
   As he, waiting, stood at the gate
That leads to the realms of Purgatory;
   (He guessed at her sorrowful fate.)

" So soon returned; thou didst not, then,
   The errand on which you went.
Didst find thy lover, and comfort him?
   Thine hour is not yet spent."

So he spoke to the wronged one, standing there,
   Sweet Ida, the spirit-maid.
No word she gave, but her shadowy arms
   Over her grieved breast laid,

With a look of despair; then whispered low,
"Let the tortures once more begin;
Let the demons bind me again to the rock,
And scourge me again for my sin!"

"And was it for this," the angel cried,
"Poor soul, that thou hast given
A thousand years, that you might have spent
In yon pure courts of heaven?

"And was it for this, that a thousand years
Were added unto thy doom?
Oh, faithful heart, a thousand years
In this region of guilt and gloom!

"'Twere better far to have suffered on,
Believing he mourned thee still,
And pining ever to soothe his grief,
Than all of thy hopes to kill

"With one fell blow! One moment, which
Brings thee but added pain.
Oh! learn, sad heart, that the dead must not
Pine for the earth again."

"Cease," cried the spirit, "I heed you not;
After that single hour
I endured on earth, e'en Purgatory
Loses its terrible power.

"After that hour," — Her shadowy form
Shook with her heart's despair, —
"After that draught of misery's dregs,
Even this gloom seems fair.

" There is little to frighten my spirit now,
    In the torturing demon's art,
For the suffering on earth, in that one brief hour,
    Hath made a hell in my heart.

" Gladly I welcome the thousand years;
    No terrors for me they own ;
I can bear them all.   What sufferings touch
    The heart that is turned to stone ! "

Her slight form swayed, her misty arms
    Stretched upward, as if she yearned
For one sweet smile to comfort her,
    From the God that her youth had spurned,

Then down she sank.   Her despairing cry
    Reached even the courts of heaven,
Where the white-robed, pure-eyed angels stood
    Touching their harps at even.

It rang thro' the realms of Purgatory,
    Till even the wretched sighed.
Over the griefs of that wrongèd one,
    As, writhing, she wailed and cried.

And was it not sad to love so well
    That neither death nor the tomb,
Nor the demons and tortures of Purgatory,
    Nor the thought of her years of doom,

Could efface from the heart one memory —
    So well that, after death,
She would brave a thousand tortures more
    To whisper one comforting breath,

And then to find but the dagger's stab?
   That this was her love's reward —
To be forgot in three month's space —
   Oh! hard was her fate, too hard!

So, even the angels in heaven's courts
   Sorrowed, if sorrow e'er
Can come to those spirits beautiful,
   In that pure, that far-off sphere.

They wept, as Seralim touched his harp
   In heaven's, choir once more,
They wept for the pains, that the spirit-maid
   For the sake of her deep love bore.

And ever the angels, leaning o'er
   Heaven's jewelled battlement,
A tear of pity, a smile of peace,
   To the heart of the maiden sent.

And ever they watched for the time when she,
   Made pure by the torturing years,
By the demons' scourges of scorpions' whips,
   By the floods of blistering tears,

Should be borne aloft, on rainbow wings
   Of the guardian spirit, prayer,
Till her fair feet pressed the steps of pearl
   That maketh to heaven a stair.

DEMETER AND PERSEPHONE.

Amid the plains of Enna, broad and fair,
   And covered o'er with tapestry of flowers,
Persephone, with Ocean's daughters played,
   Along the meads, thro' rosy flying hours.

The spring-time of the earth had kissed the land;
   With trailing garments, rainbow-hued she came;
With breath of roses, flags and hyacinths,
   And bright wild tulips, in a scarlet flame,

That rose, in perfumed odors, to the skies
   From out the censer, that she lightly swung;
While round her feet, amid the springing grass,
   The cicale's noisy chatter loudly rung.

The Northern spring is pale, but beautiful;
   She decks herself in robes of shimmering green;
But ah! she lacks the dreamful radiance
   That far in Southern lands is seen!

Her pale primroses, colorless and sweet,
   Are fair, 'tis true; but look unto the South!
Where spring-tide comes with all her rainbow hues,
   And faint, ecstatic smiles about her mouth!

Within the North, she is a fair, sweet child,
   Awakened from her darkened dreams of death;
Within the South, she wakes from dreams of love,
   Like the fair princess, whom her lover's breath,

And strong, sweet kisses, roused from her long sleep,
   To life more beautiful, to strength more strong,
To love with soundings far more wide and deep,
   That made her life one sweet, eternal song.

One comes to us with vestments of the grave,
   We welcome her as rescued from the tomb;
Like young Genevra, in her death-like trance,
   Consigned to rest within the vault's dark gloom,

Who, when life came unto her ice-touched heart,
   Arose and fled unto her lover's door,
He clasped her close, with many a soft caress, —
   So in the North, when spring-time comes once more!

But in the South! ah! there is naught on earth
   Like her sweet smile upon the Southern land!
She comes a sunbeam from the heavens above!
   Like fairy queen, she waves her magic wand;

The great, broad earth doth shake its lusty sides
   And laugh with joy to see the spring again;
While flowers bloom o'er all the lovely land,
   And from the fruit-trees fall a perfect rain

Of blooms as white as whitest driven snow,
   .That drifting with the changing, fickle wind,
In breaks of white, now laughing, come and go,
   And now, in crested waves, fall far behind.

Such time it was, when on fair Enna's plains,
   Deep-bosomed daughters of old Ocean round,
Persephone, far from her mother's care,
   Played all the day; her broad, white brow encrowned

With wreaths of flowers, woven deftly in
  A vari-colored, winding length of chain,
That graceful nymphs had gathered, as their spoils,
  This one sweet morning on fair Enna's plain.

On, on they went, in almost childish glee,
  And laughed when e'er a strange, new flower was
    found;
They plucked the blooms of wild anemoné,
  Sprung from the blood of fair Adonis' wound.

They gathered roses; this one, flushing shame,
  Upon this cheek, there sat the white despair;
While still another, maiden's-blush its name,
  Both pink and white within its bosom bare;

And great calm lilies, white as ivory,
  Where golden-winged Hymettian bees,
Grew drunk with sweetness, as our souls grow drunk
  With wine, well-flavored, long upon the lees!

There ran along the meadow, like a flame,
  Wild tulips, bright with burning, scarlet fire;
While here and there, like flecks of virgin gold,
  The knots of nodding daffodils grew nigher,

And whispered to the nestling pimpernels,
  That ope'd in wonder all their sweet blue eyes,
Which, like small mirrors, then reflected back
  The clear, deep azure of the bending skies.

Along the meadows still the young nymphs went;
  Amid the breast-high grasses, filled with gold,
And red and purple, from the countless flowers,
  That under touch of Southern sun unfold.

The gladiola, and scarlet poppy's bloom,
    The yellow crocus, that sprung in millions up,
And violets, all filled with faint perfume,
    With dew-drops nestling in each dainty cup;

The tall, plumed canes that grew beside the stream,
    Whose golden waters flowed from far-off hills;
The sheaves of arum-leaves, so soft and thick,
    Where unborn lilies slept yet, white and still;

The ocean spray of green arbutus vine;
    The tall accacia, shedding lightly down
Its silvery hair, to shield cyclamen blooms
    That nestled near its roots upon the ground.

And now they sought the purple hyacinth
    And dreamy blue of iris lilies, neath
The olive boughs and rosy almond tree,
    And lupinelli, in a tinted wreath;

And tall, strong flags of white and purple shades,
    And sweet carnations from the hillside steep.
As on they roved, their dainty, white feet sank,
    Within the beds of violets, ankle-deep.

And now Persephone, fairest of the fair,
    Beyond her young companions swift had run;
Down falling, like a veil, her wealth of hair,
    Its tresses flecked with rays from out the sun.

The velvet softness of her youthful cheek
    Grew deeper pink with unused exercise,
And mischief played around her dimpled mouth
    And shone from out the glory of her eyes;

The zone that bound her dainty, girlish waist
　　Was loosed, and from one bare arm lightly fell
The clinging robe, which only half concealed
　　The beauties of her form, she knew full well.

But who was here to mark save these, her nymphs,
　　Who followed her with purling laughter sweet,
And panting, soon gave up the merry chase,
　　As o'er the grass they watched her flying feet.

Her face half-turned across her shoulder white,
　　With dimpled hand she urged them lightly on ;
Some followed still, while others sank to rest
　　Amid a sea of early, springing corn, —

Demeter's emblem, — at Eleusian shrines,
　　Where to her honor all first-fruits were brought,
E'en on her brow she wore the yellow grain,
　　That in a crown, well-garlanded, was wrought.

Among the following was that lithe, strong nymph,
　　Fair Arethusa, one of Diana's train,
Who, frightened, fled from Alpheus' warm clasp,
　　And treated all his love with cold disdain.

And now Persephone, wearied with her flight,
　　Paused for a moment, while her nymphs drew nigh,
But spying soon a flower both new and strange,
　　To pluck it, quick her lightsome feet did fly.

'Twas the Narcissus, deadly flower, but fair ;
　　Within the Greek the emblem 'tis of death.
It sprang from earth her maiden steps to snare
　　With hundred blooms and sweetly-scented breath,

That made the sky and earth and salt wave glad.
　　It sprang to favor Aides' swift desire,
For long he'd loved the dainty, flower-like girl, —
　　This dark-browed ruler of the realms of fire!

Persephone, with tinkling laughter, drew
　　Near to the deadly, hundred-blossomed flower;
She stretched her hand to grasp the scented blooms,
　　Nor knew it held for her a deadly dower!

Her taper fingers closed upon the stalk,
　　But as she bent to break the dainty stem,
The false earth opened, and dark Aides, king
　　Of all the dead, from sulphurous caverns came!

His gloomy features, crowned with raven locks
　　That curled like serpents o'er his frown-bent brow,
His burning eyes, whence leaped the lambent flame, —
　　Ne'er had she seen such awful sight till now!

In chariot, made of solid ebony,
　　With champing steeds as dark as Erebus,
With sulphurous flames around the chariot wheels,
　　Straight had he come from realms of Tartarus!

Persephone, with frightened eyes, gazed on, —
　　No power had she to move her leadened feet;
A marble statue not more still or cold,
　　Except for fingers' swift, convulsive meet!

But now, from lips of Ocean's daughters rose
　　Affrighted screams, that tore the summer sky,
" It is, it is the face of gloomy Dis!
　　Persephone, beloved mistress, fly!

" He comes from realms of night, where Titans moan,
  Entombed in prisons 'neath his palace dark ;
From Stygian wave, where souls of dead men rove,
  'Till ferried o'er in Charon's gloomy barque.

" Stay not to gaze upon his dreadful form !
  There yet is time from his dark face to fly ! "
The maiden stood, like some poor, fluttering bird,
  That, charmèd, gazes in the serpent's eye ;

By chilling horror all her warm blood touched,
  Till thro' her veins it flowed in streams of ice.
He nearer came !   He seized her in his arms
  And held her clasped, as in an iron vice !

The white robe torn, from off her bosom fell,
  Disclosing there her ivory, globèd breasts, —
Those snowy globes of clustered beauties fair
  That tempting rose, pink-tinted at the crest.

Her yellow hair, like silken floss of corn,
  Clung round her form as if it fain would hide
Her maiden charms from Aides' fiery gaze ;
  Her deep blue eyes with fright were opened wide.

She called aloud on Zeus, high above,
  " Oh ! father, save me ! or your daughter dies ! "
But neither man nor god did answer her.
  The chariot sank ; and now the azure skies,

The rainbowed earth, the opal-tonèd sea,
  With its great waves, that moved right grandly on,
All faded from her gaze as down she sank.
  At last the beams of yellow-robèd sun

Were hid from sight, as thro' cavernous halls
    With her grim captor, — e'en more dreadful now,
Since in the darkness, her imaginings
    Saw forked tongues of flame around his brow,

Still, still she cried, in bowels of the earth,
    To her sweet mother, on Sicillia's plain;
The peaks of all the hills took up the cry,
    And depths of sea reëchoed it again.

Then Ceres heard that long, despairing cry;
    Thro' all her heart a sharp pain sudden went,
She tore the veil from off her yellow hair,
    She threw her blue hood down; afar she went,

Like to a bird amid fair Enna's fields,
    And sought her daughter 'mong the dew-kissed
        flowers.
The frightened nymphs she found, who fleeing on,
    Had hid themselves within some laurel bowers.

But still they feared to tell the bitter truth,
    Tho' weeping o'er their mistress' awful fate;
Too well they knew, dark Aides' power was such,
    They too would suffer, if they earned his hate.

Bereaved and maddened, noble Ceres went
    Forth from their presence to the flowery meads;
Soon, soon she came where turf was trampled down
    As 'twere by hoofs of strong, impatient steeds.

A fountain sprang from out the wounded earth,
    And close beside it lay her daughter's veil,
Just as it fell when, torn from off her brow,
    The gloomy master, of that nation pale,

Clasped her within his dark and brawny arms,
  And sank from earth to shades of Orcean gloom.
The noble Ceres rent her corn-like hair,
  And wildly prayed to know her daughter's doom.

The fountain answered not the mother's heart,
  Nor did the flowers smiling at her feet,
Nor bright-winged bird, that flew at evening home
  To greet his mate, safe in her nest's retreat.

In deep distress, a torch was kindlèd
  Amid the flames from Etna's burning sent,
To light her steps thro' dark ways of the world;
  So on her search, with hopeless heart she went.

Nine days she wandered o'er the bosomed earth;
  Nine days, in sorrow, still refused to taste
Divine ambrosia or the nectar sweet;
  Nine days went on, o'er rugged paths in haste!

For nine long days, all wearyful and sad,
  O'er towering mountain, sun-kissed hill and dale,
But found no trace! Until she came at last
  To Hecate, who, half hid by silver veil,

Sat evermore within her darkened cave,
  Weaving her thoughts, so pure and delicate;
Here Ceres paused, and begged the strange, dark one
  To tell if aught she knew of Kore's fate.

Then Hecate answered, "Yes, her voice I heard,
  But only that; no form, mine eyes have seen;
I know not who hath borne the maid away;
  Behind my veil, as here all day I lean,

Mine ears hear many things of many lands,
   But naught I see, oh Ceres, noble one !
Go on thy way and question Phœbus now."
   Then, saying not a word, toward the sun

She went, with blazing torch in hand ;
   As swiftly on, as e'en the arrow flies,
Until she reached the palace glorious
   Where dwelt the sun, the watchman of the skies.

Then worn with grief, and travels far and wide,
   She threw herself, in bitterest agony,
Down at his feet, and sought to know the spot,
   In earth or sky, or neath the dark blue sea,

That held her child.   He pitied her,
   And pitying told the awful story o'er ;
Her tender heart broke with this certain grief,
   And white she sank upon the golden floor.

The trance was short; the wrongèd goddess rose
   And went her way, all veiled in deepest grief
From head to foot ; around her clung her robe
   Of darkest blue, inwrought with golden leaf.

Deep anger filled her heart against the gods,
   And chief 'gainst Zeus ; so she came no more
Within the counsels of Olympus high,
   But under guise of woman, old and poor,

She veiled her beauty and her noble form,
   And wandered sad and, withal, desolate ;
Her heart all wasted with her deep regret
   And crooning evermore her daughter's fate.

Unto Eleusis, where her temples were,
  With grief-bent shoulders Ceres sadly came;
She sate her down within the temple's walls, —
  Called ever on Persephone's sweet name.

Apart from all the company divine,
  She lived on, with her wasting grief, alone;
No one to cheer, to offer nectar sweet,
  No one to soothe her daily, nightly moan!

Upon the earth a year of famine came,
  A grievous famine, by her anger sent;
The dry seed hidden laid within the soil;
  In vain the ploughshare thro' the furrow bent!

In vain the oxen drew them 'long the fields!
  In vain the seed-corn fell upon the earth!
No tender shoots sprang from the yellow grain,
  And all was famine and all was dearth!

The brazen skies looked down upon a land
  Without a sign of harvest on its slope;
All, all was bare; within the hearts of men
  There lived no more the faintest gleam of hope.

With hollow eyes, and gaunt, they dragged themselves
  Unto the temples in a famished crowd,
And prayed to Zeus, and besought him there,
  By wails of children, by their moanings loud,

To take the curse from off the blackened land;
  That in the furrows all the young green corn
Might spring again; that all the trees might bear
  Their globèd fruit; they prayed from night till
    morn.

And Zeus, high upon his awful throne,
    Heard all their prayers and pitied all their grief,
And sent the golden-sandalled Iris down;
    She fluttered to the earth like bright-hued leaf.

She bowed before the dark Eleusian shrine,
    And thus besought the hidden goddess there:
"Oh! noble Ceres, bow thine angered ear,
    And list the numbers of thy people's prayer.

"From the great Thunderer's throne I come
    To ask thy pity on the famished land.
Oh! Ceres, mother, wilt thou not return
    And sit once more amid the Olympian band?"

But Ceres turned away her tear-dimmed eyes
    From where the maiden Iris lowly bent,
And answered her with scathing, angry words:
    "Was it for this that thou wast earthward sent?

"Leave me, then, Iris, and tell to him,
    Thy Zeus great, that ne'er will I return
Unto Olympus; that earth no more shall yield
    Its fruits; for still my heart doth yearn

"For my sweet child. Let her, then, be restored!
    Then shall the earth bring forth its fruit again!
Then shall I tread Olympus' pearly floor,
    When *she* returns! But not, no, not till then!"

Meanwhile the famine grew more horrible;
    All through the land the dead by millions slept.
The living, scarce more hopeful than the dead,
    With wasted forms unto the temples crept;

Besought again the gods to take away
    The grievous famine from the weeping land.
Then earthward came still, one by one,
    The gods who round the Thunderer's footstool
        stand.

They sought to turn great Ceres from her wrath,
    But still she heard with face dark, hard, and stern;
And still her eyes, Persephone to behold,
    With strongest mother-love did yearn!

At last swift Hermes mounts the winged winds,
    Gay, golden pinions bound his feet upon,
And enters in that gloomy region dark
    Where roll the fiery waves of Phlegython.

Within his palace in that under-world,
    Within that awful, shadow-darkened home,
Where sinful dead are darkly downward hurled,
    Near fields Elysian, where just spirits roam,

The wingèd Hermes found, on ebon throne,
    Dark Aides! Near, his timid, shrinking bride,
Consumed within herself with strong desire
    To see her mother, which she could not hide!

Swift as the wings upon his hands and feet,
    The words of Hermes thro' the message fly;
Aidoneus smiles, and bids Persephone
    Prepare to go, but yields her with a sigh.

Her feet all swiftened with her depths of joy,
    She rose; within a chariot of wrought gold,
With Hermes by her side, thro' dark, infernal halls
    And shadows deep they onward rolled.

And well did Hermes guide the ebon pair;
　　And swift the coursers onward, upward ran;
And quick they went upon their journey long,
　　Till they had passed the form of Charon wan.

And now they came beyond the bounds of hell,
　　And now they passed unto the upper air;
And, as they left the realms of Tartarus,
　　With triple-headed Cerberus in his lair,

Persephone felt all her spirits rise;
　　For soon she'd greet her sorrowing mother 'gain!
That mother, who had never charmed her sight,
　　Since that spring day on blooming Enna's plain!

On, on they went; the waters of the sea
　　Resisted not, nor rivers dark and deep,
Nor black ravines among the crested hills,
　　Nor on the shore the rugged cliffs so steep,

Until at last, her glad gaze fell upon
　　Her mother's shrine, by far Eleusis' shore;
Until at last, her sandals kissed with joy
　　The marble steps without the temple's door.

The mother saw her, and so quickly ran
　　To meet her, like a dryad coming down
A mountain side, all dusky with the woods,
　　Her crocus-colored hair wild streaming round!

She clasped the lost one in her tightening arms,
　　She showered kisses on her velvet cheek;
She kissed the eyes, as clear and beautiful,
　　As limpid waters of a crystal creek!

In sweet communion all the day they sat,
   The noble Ceres and Persephone;
They told each other many a sweet-winged thought:
   Of how the mother went o'er land and sea;

Of how the daughter wept the whole day long,
   And sought sweet mercy from the gloomy Dis.
The tears came to her eyes; but Ceres bent
   And brushed them off with tender mother's kiss!

Yet still, in time of joy, remembered was
   Her vow, if to her arms her daughter came again.
She bade the earth bring forth her sweet-juiced fruits;
   She eased the people of the famine's pain.

Thro' all the land the fields were laden down
   With flowers and waving yellow corn,
And once more came the golden ears of grain,
   As in the past, her temple to adorn.

GWYN ARAUN.

Far away in the days of the Long Ago,
When the world was young; by the ceaseless flow
Of an inland river's glancing tide,
In a forest deep and dark and wide,

There lived a race, who were free from care,
Whose hearts were happy, and whose lives were fair.
Their name was Fable, these men of old,
And their age of the world was the age of gold;

And the beautiful land where they once did dwell,
With its darkened glade and its ferny dell,
Was the kingdom of Myth; and from shore to shore
It was bounded in by Fairy Lore.

No sun-rays bright, from the heaven above,
E'er pierced the veil that the forest wove
O'er the land of Myth, or the kings that reigned
In the land, ere its power and glory waned.

But deep in the heart of the forest grew
Full many a flower that was strange and new;
And feathery ferns, on many a bank
Of velvet moss, where the footfall sank;

And clear brooks ran thro' the forest deep,
Whose murmurings seemed to whisper of sleep.
Full many a year, so the story goes, —
It might have been ages, for aught one knows, —

The race of Fable lived happily on,
And the name of their prince was Gwyn Araun.
A prince so mighty, so full of power,
He knew the language of every flower;

And the great earth-secrets he learned to know.
His wisdom was such as gods bestow!
He could answer the birds, in their wildwood note,
As thro' the forest they'd lightly float;

He could talk to the stars, as gliding by
On a billowy cloud, he kissed the sky;
He would listen and hear, in the quiet night,
The words of the brook in its ceaseless flight;

He knew its music, he knew its song,
As it restless hurried its course along.
He would speak to the hoary trees, that rose
Like sentinels guarding against the foes,

And they would open their lips of wood,
And answer in language he understood;
He would sit in the forest, for many an hour,
To list to the tale of a simple flower;

And there was naught that lived in vale or dell,
But all its story he knew full well;
He would list to the weak, faint words that rise,
From the dainty lips of the butterflies;

He talked with the stars, and flowers, and trees,
And the floating clouds and the swarms of bees,
And from each and all he learned to take
Some lesson of love, for nature's sake.

He could wander unseen in any land,
And change his shape with a fairy wand;
His palace arose in a single night,
And stood in the forest, a lovely sight.

'Twas built of all that was rich and rare,
'Twas adorned with all that was bright and fair;
And there, in its gracious beauty stood,
A fairy home in a fairy wood.

He owned a horn, of ivory made,
Whose note of enchantment all obeyed;
And sorrow, and gloom, and care all fled,
To hide themselves in the ocean's bed,

When the magic blast of the ivory horn
Sounded, wild and clear, in the early morn.
So lived the prince, and his life was sweet;
Secure from the world, in his calm retreat.

But alas! one day, to the stream that flowed
By the forest deep, and dark, and broad,
There came a sage from the far-off world.
He launched his boat, and his sail unfurled,

Then over the river his course he bent,
Till safe in the harbor his craft was sent;
And then, thro' the forest moist and dark,
He followed his guide, a fire-fly spark.

So, when the shadows of evening fell,
He reached the depths of the fairy dell.
The heart of the sage was proud and cold,
And his only thought was the greed of gold.

No beauty he saw in the world around,
No music lived in the brook's sweet sound
For his deafened ear, and his steely eye
Was blind to the beauty of earth and sky;

For his was the mind of prosaic mood,
That knew not the sweetness of fancy's food,
But looked around with a soulless glance,
And pierced all things with a critic's lance.

And now, thro' the forest the sage had come
To Gwyn Araun's palace, or "Fancy's home."
Down quick to greet him the young prince stept,
As out from his lips a welcome leapt.

Ah! little he knew the sage would bring
To his cup of sweetness, a bitter sting!
Ah! little he thought his reign was o'er
In the land of Myth and of Fairy Lore!

He opened the doors of his palace fair,
And bade the stranger to enter there;
While for his sake a feast was made,
And to his presence all honor paid.

The table was graced with cups of gold,
With fine-cut goblets of dainty mould;
While flashing jewels, a king might wear,
Were set in dishes of patterns rare;

The cups of gold, entwined with vines,
Were brimming o'er with sparkling wines;
The frosted work of the goblets showed
The streams of nectar that in them flowed;

And over the jewels, the spiced meat
Lay side by side of ambrosia sweet; —
A feast where Jove and his gods might sup,
And pledge their host in a sparkling cup.

But the sage of the world, with his critic's mind,
No beauty in all the place could find.
He saw in the goblets of gold and glass,
But the acorn cups of the last year's mast,

Which held, instead of the wine's red glow,
With heart of crimson and foam of snow,
But the water dipped from the forest brook,
Where clear it wound, thro' a shady nook.

And e'en the jewelled plates, he said,
Were naught but the leaves of gold and red
Which, in the days of the autumn, fall
From their windy homes in the tree-tops tall.

Gwyn Araun listened, the hard words hurled
From the lips of the sage, we call the World,
Then slowly and sadly he turned away,
From the palace where all his treasures lay,

And mounting his magic steed at the door,
He flew from the world forevermore.
And yet sometimes, as the years roll on,
The life, the spirit of Gwyn Araun

Comes back to the earth in a poet's soul,
That lives in the form of a poet's mould.
And then again to the feast divine,
Of ambrosial food and of rosy wine,

He bids his guests.   And once again
The sage, who sees with the eyes of men,
Scoffs at the feast which the poet spreads,
And turns to the feast of the flesh instead.

And once again Gwyn Araun flies
To his poet's home, beyond the skies,
Beyond the reach of the world's cold sneers,
Beyond its sorrows, disdain, and tears.

And men go on and careless say,
" A poet died in the world to-day."
Yea, the world smiles on, tho' it sent the dart
That pierced and shivered the poet's heart.

MY FIRST LOVE.

I knew an old man, gray with many years,
His eye's strong glory dimmed with briny tears,
His furrowed face, lined o'er with hopes and fears.

He sat before his hearthstone's brilliant glow,
He watched the fire-light dancing come and go,
Now touching with its rays his head of snow,

Now making shadows on the dark gray wall,
Most quaint and weird, and most fantastical;
He watched the ashes white and lifeless fall.

No word he said, but sitting silent there,
Methought upon his spirit carked some secret care.
With tender hand I touched his silvery hair,

And whispered in the darkness, "Tell, I pray,
What thoughts of life brood o'er thy heart to-day?"
I plead with him, nor did he say me nay.

" My child, my thoughts to-night are in the past, —
Of my first love, who went from me so fast, —
My first, my only love, my last!"

With all the eager, seeking heart of youth,
With all its selfish joy in other's ruth,
I said, " Pray tell the tale; its truth

" Will make it sweet unto my listening ears ;
Then haste, repeat this tale of early years!"
He sighed, and in his sigh was sound of tears.

" My first love! what dear, sweet memories crowd
   Around the day when first I met her, proud
   To know her then, and sing her praises loud.

" Too young was I the real love to know,
   That, river-broad, which thro' the heart doth flow,
   Which asketh nothing, yet doth all bestow.

" Too young as yet; but craving others' love
   And praises sweet, on which my young heart throve,
   Until at last, I reached that bliss above

" All others, when all things equal are, —
   That time remembered in the days afar
   As the first dawning of life's morning star, —

" The time one loves, and is beloved again,
   Can give and take without one thought of pain,
   When ' happiness ' is all life's sweet refrain.

" That blissful time our hearts but once conceive,
   When love we give, and equally receive,
   With ne'er a thought of harm, or to deceive.

" My child, that time of happiness I've known,
   And of its blissful hours, tho' all have flown,
   As from the broken lute the music's tone,

" Still comes the thought, that naught can take away,
   I loved and was beloved like this one day,
   Alas! the time's sweet blisses could not stay!

" How lovely all the throbbing, living world!
   How blue the banners that the skies unfurled!
   How fair the earth by silver moon impearled!

4

" How fresh and balmy all the spring-time air,
   When hand in hand, unconscious yet of care,
   I wandered with my first love, bright and fair!

" Where'er we went, o'er field, in shaded grove,
   All nature laughed upon me and my love,
   And swift to please us every creature strove.

" Joy smiled to greet us, in her blithesome way,
   And Pleasure took our hands and bade us stay,
   While Music welcomed with a merry lay!

" Lo, thus we went, with laughter and with smiles,
   Far thro' the world, o'er verdant, flowery miles,
   Free from all sorrow or sin-touching guiles.

" We sang for joy, and older ones would turn
   And look upon us, first with eyes half stern;
   But then our merry youth they would discern;

" The eyes would soften, and we'd hear them say:
  ' So young, so happy, let them go their way;
   When *we* were young, thus did we lightly stray!'

" Then, with a smile, and oft a tender sigh,
   They'd pass along, while we, thro' fields of rye
   And waving grain, so bearded, brown, and high,

" Would laugh and sing; too happy in the thought
   Of mutual, deepening love, to care for aught
   In all the world, except the joy we sought.

" She clung to me with such a loving glance, —
   That look e'en now my broken spirit haunts, —
   She pressed me to her in the circling dance;

"And in my heart I did not once conceive
That she could e'er grow cold, could ever leave
Me to my fate. Alas! our dreams deceive!

"Days, weeks, and months, and years passed by;
They brought no change of love to her. And I
Lived with her happy; but a change was nigh!

"One evening,—shall I e'er forget that fateful day,
When like a maddened animal at bay,
I felt, yea knew, 'My love will go away!'

"All morn our thoughts had happily flowed on,
But when there came the twilight, gray and wan,
It seemed that something from the hour was gone!

"I turned to where my love was standing; bold
I seized her hand, but it was strangely cold!
I shuddered, and an icy fear o'er all my spirit rolled.

"Beneath my breath I whispered, soft and low,
'My love, my love will leave me soon I know!'
With aching heart I wandered to and fro.

"I sought within her eyes, that once were wont
To turn their light to mine, as to their font,
Some look of hope, or e'en a burning taunt,

"To tell me why this coldness of her heart;
But none she gave, and evermore apart
Our sad lives grew. Sometimes, with sudden start

"And passion wild, she'd strain me to her breast;
Upon my lips again her kisses would be pressed;
She'd laugh again, as if with old-time zest.

" But her kisses' sweetness was lost forevermore ;
  All her love and laughter were hollow at the core ;
  Her passion did not thrill me, as once it did of yore.

" And then with swift, unkind, averted gaze,
  She'd push me from her side ; for days and days
  Would 'gain enstrange my heart with careless
    ways.

" I saw, alas ! she wished my love no more ;
  When I caressed her, from my arms she tore
  Her graceful form ; yet all I sadly bore !

" One even, weary, sad, I entered in
  The home, where once my happiest hours had
    been, —
  Alas ! those hours have never come again !

" The room was dark ; it's very hearth was cold ;
  Around my heart, with grasp so icy cold,
  I felt some strange, sad thing relentless fold.

" I fell to earth and shook with awful fear ;
  I tried to weep, but not a single tear
  Came to my eyes ; the balls were hot and sere.

" In agony more deep, more fierce, more wild,
  Than ever comes to old man or to child,
  I writhed ; no voice of reason mild

" Came all my grief to calm ; I only felt the pall
  Of her desertion ; my life, my love, my all,
  Had gone from me, beyond my love's recall.

" From that time, all my life has bitter grown ;
  For me, the lute has lost its music's tone ;
  For her, in secret, do I make my moan.

" I tried to show a happy, mirthful face,
   But could not hide my sorrow's bitter trace,
   That robbed my life of all its crowning grace.

" At last I wearied of the pretence vain,
   And tried no more to hide my secret pain,
   For my sweet love did never come again !

" I know that naught can bring her back to me,
   With all her love, so happy and so free !
   No more her face of beauty shall I see !

" Yet for my first love still I sometimes weep;
   Sometimes she comes to me, in dreams of sleep,
   And then, in dreams, my soul I wish to steep !

" I miss her every hour in every day.
   For but one moment do I fondly pray, —
   One moment ! I would make it then alway !

" I'd give — oh God ! what thing would I not give
   Through all these blissful hours once more to live ?
   My love, can you my agony conceive ?

" Oh ! all that I possess of earthly store,
   Each joy of mine I'd give, could they restore
   My love, that I might call her mine once more ! "

   The tale was ended ; the embers' fitful glow
   Had darkened, died, and left the ashes snow ;
   The old man sat with head bowed down and low.

   I said, " It is, indeed, a tale of grief and ruth, —
   Now tell me who the maiden was, in sooth ? "
   He whispered low, " My child, she was my Youth ! "

THE GOLDEN CELANDINE.

In the age, when the fairies lived on earth,
When the wildwood rang with their songs of mirth,
As they danced 'neath the branching greenwood
    tree,
And laughed aloud in their merry glee,

There lived a shepherd lad, whose life
Was full of sorrow, and grief, and strife.
It chanced that the shepherd roved one day,
At dewy eve, in the month of May,

Away from his flocks on the breezy hill,
To a shady wood, where the wind was still.
There he sate him down, in his deep despair,
For his heart was heavy and full of care.

As thus he sat, at the twilight hour,
A fairy came, with a golden flower
In her dainty hand, so white and small,
That it hardly seemed like a hand at all.

She gave him the blossom, and whispered low,
"Cheer up, sad heart, this secret know:
Breathe thrice on this bloom of Celandine,
And thrice you shall have your wish, I ween!"

So saying, the fairy winged her flight;
And the shepherd lingered till shades of night
Came down on the wood, and folded it all
In the awful shroud of its darkening pall,

Then slowly arose and wended his way,
And thought on the gift of the forest-fay.
He half-way doubted the words she said,
And to breathe on the flower was half afraid;

But still in his fingers he held it fast,
And, doubting, breathed on the bloom at last.
And wishing to see if the gift was true,
"Oh! grant that I laugh as others do!"

So, e'en as he wished, he laughed aloud;
His voice was merry in every crowd,
And he laughed o'er a flagon of glorious wine;
But he lacked in his laughter the touch divine,

Which maketh the sweetness of joy alone,
As the deep chord maketh the music's tone;
So the lad grew sick of his joyless mirth;
And counted his laughter as little worth.

Then he breathed again on the yellow bloom,
So heavily laden with rich perfume,
" Let me love as others do," he said,
" No more of mirth, —give me love instead ! "

Then a maiden came, with starry eyes,
That were lifted to his in a sweet surprise;
Pressed the coral curves of her lip's red bow
To his; and gave him her hand of snow.

But it seemed to him that her lips were cold;
Her bright eyes dim, and the faultless mould
Of her dainty figure was but the grace,
That is seen in the statue's form and face.

Now twice he had owned his heart's desire, —
The tones of laughter and love's swift fire;
But his heart was hungered; he was not content,
So sadly again o'er the flower he bent,

Then breathed, with a sigh, in its golden heart,
And said to his laughter and love, " Depart;
Your joy and passion are not for me.
The fairy's gift and its golden key

" I give to others, that their mirth and love
May make earth sweet as the realms above ! "
Then sighing and weeping, he cast the flower
Down to the earth, with its fairy dower.

But, strange to say, his heart grew light;
And the world was beautiful in his sight;
He sang aloud in his rapture sweet;
The hours once long were now too fleet;

The maiden who stood beside him there,
With the sunlight flecking her waving hair,
Was fair in his eyes, and her lips were far
More warm than the suns of summer are;

And the kisses he stole from her dewy mouth,
Were sweeter than winds that blew from the South.
Then the fairy came, with happiest mien,
And raising the golden Celandine,

" Since all that you wished was others' joy,
And pure from a selfish greed's alloy,
Now laughter is yours, and love," she said,
As far on the evening breeze she sped.

TWICE-TOLD.

How happy poets must have been
 In early days of earth ;
I envy them their tears and smiles,
 Their half-way childish mirth.

The days of youth the old world knew
 Must sure have sweetest been ;
They knew so little, and they yet
 Were happiest of men !

What joy to work, not knowing half
 The secrets of your art !
And then to feel, with sudden touch,
 Th' Inspirer in your heart !

With always something to be won,
 Some goal that ne'er was gained,
Some secrets, none had ever pierced,
 Some throne, where none had reigned.

Like to some venturous traveller, who
 Seeks far in new-found lands,
The pleasure, he could never feel
 Upon his native strands.

But now, alas ! what glory's left ?
 The glory of the past !
For Art's pure blossoms wither now
 Before grim Science's blast.

And now! what is there left to do?
  For all has been twice told.
The unknown ocean, tempting on,
  That for Columbus rolled,

Has been traversed by many a sail, —
  And so it is with song;
Its surging billows now are calmed,
  Its treasures rifled long.

'Tis true, if such our feeble wish,
  We may upon its waves
Trust our small craft, and rest at last
  Upon the sands it laves.

But what of that?   The glories which
  The earlier seamen drew
Have been all told, in words more sweet
  Than modern verse e'er knew.

All has been painted, sung, and said;
  The tales are all twice-told;
And Inspiration touches not
  The hands that work for gold.

All has been painted, — not a shade
  The modern artist gives
To warm his picture into life,
  But in Leonardo lives.

And tho' thro' many a weary day
  The painter toils for gold,
His canvas shames him in the end, —
  The tale has been twice-told!

All has been sculptured, chiselled fair,
   From out the marble cold ;
We turn away, and sighing, say,
  "The tale has been twice-told!"

All has been sung, — no poet now
   Doth touch with note divine,
But what, among the masters great,
   The sparkling thought we find.

No more is left for modern song ;
   No beauties to unfold.
How sad, alas! those dreary words,
  "The tale has been twice-told."

And oh! with what a weary heart
   We pine against our doom,
And envy those who picked the buds,
   And watched them burst to bloom.

God grant that when our spirits speed
   Beyond the sunset's gold,
We then may taste those joys of love
   Which never are twice-told!

LILLITH.

Whene'er I hear the magic name,
　　And she the name doth bear,
Like Lillith of the olden days,
　　Hath braids of dead-gold hair,

I think of that weird Jewish tale,
　　Within the Talmud old, —
That cavern deep, which, dark and grim,
　　Doth jewels rare enfold, —

The tale of Lillith, she who lived,
　　The Jewish legends tell,
Within the shades of Eden's bowers
　　Ere Adam, tempted, fell;

Ere yet, indeed, the gentle Eve,
　　With tender, loving heart,
Filled with a sweet humility,
　　Formed of his life a part.

For, "Lillith of the golden hair,"
　　To Adam first was given
To be his wife, — a gift most fair,
　　Bestowed by kindest heaven.

Methinks I see her standing now
　　Within the groves of Paradise,
Her snow-white lids just sloping down
　　To hide the flash of royal eyes, —

Those eyes! great, glowing, purple stars,
  That sink within the soul,
As, throwing back the fringèd lids
  With woman's swift control,

She turns them, all their purple shades
  Grown darker, to your face;
A scornful smile her red lips move,
  And curving round them plays.

A creature most superbly made,
  So tall and strong and white;
Her skin, as fair as milky curds,
  Glowed 'neath the sunshine bright.

Her graceful limbs perfection were;
  Her firm chin's rounded curve,
Showed her a creature of less heart
  Than manly strength of nerve.

With not a crinkle in its thread,
  In waves of molten gold,
From sunny brow and well-set head
  Her hair's rich glory rolled;

Like some curbed river, breaking bonds
  And rushing madly down,
The tresses all-tumultuous fell
  Her strong, lithe form around.

So, in the legend she is called,
  "Lillith the golden haired,"—
How many a Lillith since that day
  The hearts of men have snared!

But tho' so fair to outward view,
   Within her purple eyes,
So glorious with their darkening shades,
   A sleeping demon lies!

So proud, so stern, so hard, so cold,
   The glorious Lillith grew,
That Adam, tired of daily strife,
   Far from her presence flew,

And prayed the Lord to take away
   This wife, with tongue as keen,
And temper fierce and wayward as
   The temper of a fiend.

'Twas done, and Lillith lived no more,
   Within pure Paradise;
Another face, as fair as hers,
   With tender, soulful eyes,

Was now the magnet sweet that moved
   The depths of Adam's love,
And showed him heaven on earth below,
   As sweet as that above.

She loved her lord, and loving felt
   Her cup filled to the brim;
In Milton's words, " He lived for God,
   And she for God in him!"

All day, far thro' the quiet glades,
   And by the streams that flowed
Thro' many a broad and flowery mead
   In the garden of the Lord,

The couple roved; and Adam, scarce
   Remembering now that one
Of glorious form and yellow hair,
   Like rays from out the sun,

Was happy; ever loving more
   That sweet, low voice of hers,
Which with its artless, merry tones,
   His inmost being stirs.

But what of Lillith, banished one
   From Eden's wide domain?
Her fierce, wild spirit fiercer grew
   With all her jealous pain;

For tho' a fiend in human shape,
   A woman's heart was still
Within her breast, e'en tho' her head
   Possessed a demon's will.

True to her devilish nature, soon
   Does crafty Lillith take
The serpent's horrid, slimy form;
   And for sweet vengeance's sake,

She tempts, with lies as black as night,
   That pure and guileless one,
Who ne'er before had any act
   Of evil thought or done.

And Lillith, crafty, cruel, cold,
   Laid all her plans too well;
For ah! we know the mournful tale
   Of how our Mother fell!

Still more the Jewish legend tells
　　Of Lillith's demon wiles;
How to this day, she roves on earth,
　　And tempts men with her smiles.

And if they yield ! God help them then !
　　For she no pity hath;
Behind those pleasing, siren ways
　　There lurks a demon's wrath !

And when they die, the legend tells,
　　Around their hearts, so cold,
Is twined a long and dainty thread
　　Of Lillith's hair of gold.

THE VINTAGE HYMN.

Oh! bring me the bindweed and fig,
   The fir, the ivy, and vine;
And I, to the sound of your dancing feet,
   A crown for Bacchus will twine.

This is the time of the vintage;
   Under the arbors there,
Groweth the clustering grape,
   Purple as Mænad's hair, —

Groweth the clustering grapes,
   Sun of the summer hath kissed;
Glowing in his caresses,
   To passionate amethyst.

Hanging, like drops of nectar
   Sucked by the sweet-tongued bees,
Who come in the days of August
   In golden argosies,

To swing on the purpling clusters,
 'Neath the shadowy, swaying vine,
Till they dream no more of the flowers,
 Drunk with this glorious wine.

Oh! the joys of the vintage!
 Laugh to your heart's content,
Mid the vines on the hillside,
 Sweet with the marvellous scent

That rises from grapes all bruisèd,
 Shedding their tears of blood;
Deep in the old wine-presses
 Floweth the crimson flood,—

Floweth the wine, that kisses
 Lips with a deeper glow,
And stirreth the heart of the lover,
 Till like to its dark red flow,

His heart's blood quickens and flies,
 On with a tumult's roll,
Till he dreams in the wildest dreamings
 Of the maiden dear to his soul.

Oh! the joy of the vintage!
 Treading a measure sweet,
We laugh 'neath the darkening shadows;
 Onward the maddening feet!

Dancing, entrancing, and glancing,
   This is the fruit we treasure ;
Onward ye youths and maidens,
   Dance to the magical measure !

Dance to the sweet midsummer,
   Days of the grape and the vine,
When floweth in the wine-presses
   The maddening, scarlet wine !

Deep in the amber-crushed nectar,
   Fill all your cups to the brim !
" Drink to the one that loves you ! "
   This be our vintage hymn !

Sweet, my love, who standeth,
   Shadows about thy feet,
Drink to the heart that loves you,
   Since goeth the days so fleet !

Fair art thou, and graceful
   As tendril of clinging vine ;
Crimson thy lips are glowing,
   Like to the royal wine ;

Purple thine eyes' dark shadows,
   Glowing with golden glint,
Like to the amber that mingles
   In with the amethyst tint.

Since thine eyes are like to the grape,
   And thy lips to the glorious wine,
Rest but thine eyes upon me !
   Press but thine lips to mine !

Madder my heart blood's beating,
   Than the rythmic measure I beat,
Drunker were I with kisses,
   Than with the grape-blood sweet.

But since thou wilt not kiss me,
   Nor raise those eyes to mine,
Raise to thy lips the nectar,
   And pledge me in cup of wine!

For the days of the golden October
   Are passing, quick passing away ;
Tho' the sun is still white in the valleys,
   Where the shadows are sleeping alway.

Tho' the crocuses yellow are blooming,
   The violets now are missed ;
And far o'er the brim of the mountains
   Are clouds of deep amethyst.

Tho' the gardens are filled with odors,
   So sweet, of the damask rose ;
Yet early, in hours of morning,
   Over the hillside glows

That mist of crimson and amber,
    That telleth of winter frost ;
While deep in the depths of the valley
    The reddening leaves are tossed.

From the hills, in pomp of scarlet
    And purple, and gold and bronze,
To the brook that floweth beside them,
    'Tween feathery, ferny fronds,

All speak of the winter that cometh
    When October is faded and gone,
When the hoar frost toucheth the sloping
    Of upland and of lawn.

When the grapes are all bruised and broken,
    When no more the dancing feet,
Nor voices of men and maidens,
    Sing of the vintage sweet.

Then plunge in the foaming nectar
    And fill to the brim thy cup !
To Bacchus, the king of the vintage,
    Our hymn we will offer up !

HOW CAME THE ARTS.

So long as our first parents happy lived
   Within the beauteous glades of Paradise, —
So long as they, remembering His command,
   Lived with His fear before their truthful eyes, —

So long they knew what meaneth "perfect rest,"
   With not a single wish of heart denied ;
With faultless nature's every beauty blest,
   And not a thought of soul unsatisfied.

Within that Eden's hills and valleys wide,
   That everlasting garden of delight,
No hint of imperfection shocked the eye,
   But all was lovely to the charmèd sight.

What need of art in such a world as this,
   Of poet's song or work of painter's brush,
When nature filled the soul with perfect bliss,
   And threw o'er all a holy music's hush ?

What needed they of music, when the world
　Was one unbroken chord of symphonies,
That to their souls sang ever, night and day,
　Like to that music where God's spirit is?

Like to those notes, so very sweet,
　They'll fill our souls with tears,
When freed from earth's cold bonds of sense,
　We rest among the spheres.

What needed they of poets and their art,
　Or any rythmic, measured lines of song,
When their own lives, of purest happiness,
　Were unwrit poems, perfect, sweet, and long?

When round them, in the very air they breathed,
　Replete with thousand joys, perfection given,
Was poetry itself, intense, sublime, —
　The very essence, straight from spheres of heaven.

What needed they of painting glorious tints?
　No Titian, Guido, or e'en Claude Lorraine,
'Ere touched the canvas with such lights and shades,
　As greeted them on every smiling plain

Of their fair-spreading, happy Paradise ;
　So beautiful that, fallen as we are,
Our wildest dreams of all its loveliness
　Are far from it, as earth from furtherest star.

What needed they, amid primeval woods,
  To raise on high grand architectural piles,
With thousand spires, heaven-kissing,
  And sweet, dim gloom amid its winding aisles,

When over-arching branches wove above
  A canopy, more beautiful by far,
Than in some old Cathedral, quaint and dim,
  The loveliest frescoings of the pencils are ?

What needed they of sculptor's patient art,
  From out the senseless marble, white and cold,
To chisel forms, that seem to step from out
  A marble curtain in a human mould ?

What needed they of these poor works of man, —
  When, ever true and faithful to the line
Of graceful curves and beauty's sense innate,
  They lived themselves, — the human form di-
    vine ? —

That form, which was perfection in itself.
  Our fallen nature never e'en conceives
Its god-like beauty, tho' we gaze upon
  The work of Phidias or Praxiteles.

But from this spot, — perfection's own sweet home, —
  Where grace, and beauty, and fair innocence
Lived ever, breathing happiness complete
  On every thought of soul or wish of sense,

They fell.   No words are needed more, —
　　No need to paint their sorrows and their sighs,
As o'er their souls rolled one great grief, —
　　Farewell to all their beauteous Paradise!

To us, their children, come still beauteous dreams
　　Of some lost world in which our spirits dwelt,
Ere' round our souls ethereal, the bars
　　And sensual bonds of carnal flesh were felt ;

Visions of beauty, that float in mystic grace
　　Around our lives and thro' the busy brain ;
But though we concentrate our every thought,
　　And quick to hold them, every strong nerve strain,

We find, alas! too often, that our dreams —
　　Or maybe memories of the skies —
Of what our souls might once have been
　　Ere they lost Paradise,

Flee from us, like the clouds of mist
　　That every grasp elude,
And melt into the ether blue
　　When touched by hands too rude.

But evermore those visions haunt
　　The artist's spirit eyes,
And evermore he struggles on,
　　Those dreams to realize.

He often fails to reach their heights,
   But think you that the less
He loves to seek untiring for
   The ideal loveliness?

'Tis this that makes, for fallen man,
   Those arts that teach the soul
To link, in common with its own,
   Each heart, from pole to pole.

'Twas this that gave the fine arts rise,—
   This craving of the mind,
To throw aside the iron bars
   In which it is confined;

And rising from its prison walls,
   Its soul to gratify
With inspiration that have less
   Of earth in them than sky.

The glorious harmonies of verse,
   The master poet sings,
Are but the echoes he would touch,
   Had but his spirit wings.

The great musician struggles e'er
   To touch the music notes
Which, sweet with heaven-born symphonies,
   Thro' all his spirit floats.

And if the poet paints in words
    His half-forgotten dreams,
The painter speaks in all his works
    More wisdom than he deems;

And when from sculptor's toiling hand
    The marble forms arise,
We know his soul was steeped within
    The dreams of Paradise.

THE LEGEND OF THE LUCCIOLA.

In a garden, dim with the twilight's pall,
    And dusky with shadow of trees,
Where the jasmine vine, all tangled and fine,
    Swayed slow in the southern breeze,

While its golden bells, with their musical knells,
    Kept ringing their half-sad chimes,
And the incoming winds, from the far away pines,
    Flowed sweeter than poet's rhymes;

Where the queen of the night, cape-jasmine white,
    All redolent with perfume,
Sat pure and alone on her emerald throne,
    With a grace she alone can assume!

Where magnolias' creamy buds unfold,
    And their rose-flushed arrows fall;
Where the mock-bird sings thro' the summer-night,
    From its nest in the tree-top tall; —

In this dim old garden, far away,
  I lived in my childhood's hours,
And heard the music that nature gives,
  And learned the songs of the flowers.

And oft, when the summer nights had come,
  And the garden ways were still,
And the Southern moon, with its yellow light,
  Hung low on the crest of the hill,

I wandered amid the wealth of blooms,
  And listened with childish fear,
To the sad, sad moan of the whippoorwill,
  That sounded now far, now near!

And watched the fire-flies restless go
  From the glory into the gloom,
Like well-spent lamps, whose lights go out
  In the darkness of the tomb.

And far adown the garden path,
  Where the vines grew thick and damp,
I followed fast in their fairy train,
  To catch but one golden lamp.

When safe in the pink of my tiny palm
  The quivering fire-fly lay,
I gazed awhile at the burning spark,
  Then loosed it to fly away.

Away, away, on the wings of the wind !
  Where the fairy queen did dwell,
In a little nook, beside the brook,
  I had named the fairies' dell.

For, firm in the faith of fairy lore,
  I believed that the fire-flies all
Were tiny sprites of the summer nights,
  Who danced at the fairies' ball.

And that evermore in the garden old,
  They swung their lanterns bright,
As they danced in the magic circle round,
  'Neath the rays of the pale moonlight.

    *   *   *   *   *   *   *   *

The years passed on, and once again
  I stood in the garden old,
On a fair, soft night I shall ne'er forget,
  When summer was just half-told.

The moon hung over the darkening hill,
  As she used in the days gone by,
And far away in the whispering pines,
  I heard the whippoorwill's cry.

The jasmine vine, all tangled and fine,
  Climbed up to the balcony roof;
Its warp all wreathed of emerald leaves,
  And its golden bells for the woof.

The garden-lilies, all white without,
  But hearts of gold within,
Were nodding along the bordered paths,
  At the breath of the southern wind.

The red oleanders crimson glowed,
  Far down the darkened ways,
And called to mind the memories
  Of childhood's happy days.

The wild pomegranate's blushing flowers,
  The myrtle with dew-drops wet,
And the fair magnolia's waxen cups,
  In their emerald canopies set,

All brought me back the summer night
  When, in this garden old,
I saw the fire-flies dancing go,
  And watched their lamps of gold.

Then, smiling at the strange conceit,
  I turned to where he leaned
Beside me in the summer night,
  His handsome face half-screened,

And told him o'er my childish thought;
  How, ever thro' the night,
These winsome fairies, one and all,
  Swinging their lanterns bright,

Went on their paths beneath the boughs,
  At the sound of the cricket's call,
To dance away, until break of day,
  At the queen of the fairies' ball.

He laughed a long, low, merry laugh,
  And bent his glowing eyes
Upon my face, but did not mark
  The crimson blushes rise.

" That is a tale for childish ears."
  But know you not the truth
Of what the " Lucciole " are ? —
  My tale is meant for youth ! —

The " Lucciola," thus they call
  The fire-fly's burning gleam,
Within the fair Italian land,
  Where burning millions teem

Thro' all the dusky summer nights,
  And almost put to shame
The oleanders' dark red glow,
  With all their crimson flame.

Once, on a night in sultry June,
  When, glowing like sparks of gold,
They burned beneath the olive boughs,
  I heard the legend told;

By one, with eyes of luminous dark,
   Whose mouth was like a rose,
Who leaned from out the casement white,
   With a graceful Southern pose,

And gleaned them from acanthus coils,
   Within her hair to set;
And there they glimmered, glowed, and died
   Amid her coils of jet.

Long years ago, when Eros reigned
   Throughout this flowery land,
He floated often, thro' the night,
   By every sea-breeze fanned,

To every rose-crowned balcony
   Where lute's sweet music thrilled,
And listened to the burning words
   That oft the music stilled, —

Those tender words that lovers speak
   In the lustrous, moonlight rays,
When soft sighs tremble to the lips,
   And love speaks in the gaze!

When burning hands are folded fast,
   And all else is forgot
Save this, that love hath found them now
   Who once thought love was not.

6

And listening to those love-words sweet,
    He thought, " How sad it seems
That things so beautiful should die,
    Or live on but in dreams.

" These murmuring, burning, tender words,
    Sure they should deathless be ;
For their sweet sound is e'en as old
    As all eternity.

" And yet they seem so new, so new,
    And lovers love them still,
And ever in the summer night
    Of love-words drink their fill.

" See, then, that I, whom men call Love,
    Will give these sweet words wings ;
Their fire shall burn in them like stars, —
    These heavenly, holy things ! "

Thus Eros spoke, and on the night
    The winged words were flung ;
And to this day the legend is
    By many a lover sung.

Therefore the " Lucciole " gleam
    Thro' all the summer nights ;
Year after year their fitful fires
    Burn in a million flights.

So thus for evermore they live,
   These passion-sparks of life,
The living fires of love, that burn
   When summer airs are rife.

They shine, like fallen stars, among
   The waving fields of grain ;
They sparkle o'er the bending grass,
   Like drops of golden rain.

But rocking on the rose's breast,
   Or in the vines above,
They are living words of passion,
   To prove the truth of love.

Let him who doubts the legend
   But walk abroad to-night,
And see the red oleander
   Grow paler by their light ;

And see them light to flaming
   Magnolia's creamy cup,
All filled with odorous perfumes
   To Flora offered up ;

Or resting, like to rubies,
   Within the lily's heart,
Until they, to her whiteness,
   Their burning fires impart ;

When the lute has hushed its music,
And two loving shadows lean
In the dark shades of the ilex, —
He will doubt no more, I ween.

THE FOUR SAINTS.

In the long ago, — so the story runs,
  In a legend quaint and old, —
Four saints of heaven were given the task
  Four nations of earth to mould.

And one was the patron of England's isle,
  And one of the land of France, —
St. George, who quelled the dragon fierce ;
  St. Denis, with sword and lance.

St. Jago is held in reverence due
  'Mid the sunny hills of Spain ;
St. Michael's name is chanted most
  In Italy's sweet refrain.

They had stood in the courts of heaven all day,
  With idle and folded wings ;
Their duty was now to make for earth
  Four nations of living things.

So first St. George, with a master hand,
   Took a piece of the purest gold,
And buried it deep in a lump of lead;
   Then down to the earth it rolled,

And fell in the lap of Albion's land,
   So oft by the poets sung;
From the lump of lead, with its heart of gold,
   The English people sprung.

St. Jago filled a bladder with wind,
   Till it puffed and swelled so wide, —
Then he placed therein the heart of a fox,
   And the fang of a wolf that had died.

Down to the earth these things he sent,
   O'er many a mountain and plain,
Till they rested beyond the Pyrenees,
   And became the people of Spain.

St. Denis, so light and free of heart,
   Turned him toward the sun,
And caught from there a flying beam,
   Whose journey had just begun.

He tied it with knots of ribbon bright,
   And sent it to earth with a glance;
It came like the gleam of a falling star,
   And fell on the land of France.

But alas! he was careless, nor thought to give
    The ballast to keep it right;
So the sunbeam proved, in the hearts of men,
    Too fragile a thing, and light.

And the knot of ribbons, so deftly tied,
    Were omens of ill, not good;
They were brilliant, true, but deeply dyed
    In hues of the crimson blood.

Now Michael, watching with eyes so keen,
    Saw errors the others had wrought,
And turned to his task with a prayer on his lips,
    And his soul brimming o'er with thought.

Like Denis, he caught a sunbeam too,
    All brilliant and undefiled,
The ringing chords of a soft-toned lute,
    And the heart of a little child,

The passionate kiss of a lover's mouth,
    A dark-eyed poet's sighs,
A silver string from an angel's lyre,
    And a rose out of Paradise;

Then, with them all in his hand, he went
    And knelt at the Father's throne,
And prayed him, saying, " My work is done,
    Except for one thing alone.

"Oh! make it perfect, that man may be
    No creature of earthly sod!
All that I ask, oh! Father mine,
    For him, is a smile of God!"

The Father smiled; so the good saint sent
    His fair work down to the earth;
And the smile and the sigh and the music gave
    Italia's children birth.

But alas! it happened that Satan, bold,
    Watched at the gates of Hell,
And saw the work, so beautiful,
    As from walls of Heaven it fell.

He said to himself, in his wicked heart,
    "If his work unspoilèd be,
'Twill make an Eden upon the earth,
    In the land called Italy!"

So he drew his bow, and an arrow sped
    That was black with a poisoned dart;
It cleft the flower from Paradise,
    And wounded the child's pure heart;

But the poet's sigh it did not touch,
    Nor the lover's kiss of fire,
Tho' it broke with a twang the silver string,
    That came from the angel's lyre.

But tho' to this day there rankles still,
  In the burning Italian heart,
The arrow that Satan sent from Hell,
  With its horrible, poisoned dart,

The smile, that God in his goodness gave,
  Still lingers within his eyes,
As if he saw in fancy yet
  The rose out of Paradise.

THE MODERN ARACHNE.

'Tis June; those sleepy, drowsy days,
　When one can sit for hours,
And weave a thousand rosy dreams,
　Among the odorous flowers.

Upon a long, low portico,
　With downward sloping eaves,
Where tangled vines of jasmine
　And honeysuckle wreathes,

We sit and while the morning hours,
　My lady fair and I;
I watch her taper fingers swift,
　As back and forth they fly,

Netting the dainty, flaxen threads
　In a bit of filmy lace, —
Now swift, now slow, they come and go, —
　Like the threads the spiders trace.

Sitting here in the summer morn,
    I watch, as the thread she plies,
Robed in a lavender muslin fine,
    That matches her violet eyes,

With the rays of sunlight creeping in
    Through the swaying, tangled vine,
Playing amid her curls of gold,
    And flushing her cheeks like wine;

Touching their waxen, rounded curves,
    Dancing now out, now in;
Resting at last, with a satisfied air,
    In the cleft of her dimpled chin.

I watch and wonder, to see her weave
    With fingers so white and deft,
That the spider, who hangs in the vines above,
    Must deem herself bereft

Of her lifetime skill by this maiden here,
    Weaving in tracery fine,
The dainty filaments into lace,
    In many a web-like line.

As I watch, I ponder the legend o'er
    Of Arachne, of olden time,
Whose sorrowful fate, in schoolboy days,
    I had read in Ovid's rhyme.

How the Lydian maiden's sinful pride,
  In what was an evil hour,
Urged her to challenge Athena stern,
  To a trial of spinning power.

But alas! for Arachne, tho' she spun
  Her finest, filmiest mesh,
The goddess of wisdom brooked not defeat
  From the hands of a maid of flesh!

And angered that mortals should even dare
  To rival the work she'd spun,
She tore with her hands the dainty web
  With which Arachne won,

And snatching a spoke from out the wheel,
  She smote the forehead fair
Of her Lydian rival, who hanged herself,
  In the depths of her heart's despair.

But Pallas, relenting, staid her weight
  Ere the spark of life was gone,
And turning her into a spider, said,
  " Thou mayest live and still spin on!"

I smile at the legend, and wonder if
  Some lover, with mistress sweet,
Had looked from the spider, spinning o'er
  Her silvery web so neat,

To his lady fair, as she spun and wove
  The flax, with its golden thread,
In a dainty woof, that seemed as fine
  As the spider's gossamer shred,

And then, from fancies within his brain,
  This tale of a poet's thought
About the spider that hangs in air,
  With a poet's license wrought.

I wonder, again, if the maiden wore
  A lavender muslin dress ;
If her eyes were purple as violets,
  And golden her crinkling tress ;

If she sat demurely beneath the vines,
  Where the rays of sunlight dance,
And tangled his heart in a seamless web
  With the magical threads of her glance, —

In a seamless mesh, as finely spun
  And soft as the gossamer lines,
The spider is weaving about her prey
  Up there in the jasmine vines.

But stronger by far than iron gyves,
  They chain and fetter her slave ;
In vain will he strive to throw them off,
  There's nothing his heart can save !

And so with me, as I lazily dream
Here in the summer sun,
My heart ensnared in a tangled web
That the violet eyes have spun !

THE LAST DAY OF SUMMER.

Again upon the hillsides come
   The scarlet, bronze, and gold ;
Again at early morn we feel
   The wind blow keen and cold ;

But the first chill crispness of the dawn
   Melts in the radiant day,
With all the scent and summer warmth,
   That speaks of summer's stay.

The misty haze, that floats above
   The mountain's distant brim,
Lights 'neath the sun-ray's kisses warm,
   And melts in distance dim.

The clear, cold air of early morn
   Grows warmer 'mid the trees,
Until its keenness sinks and dies
   Into a soft sea-breeze.

The radiance of the cloudless day,
    The earthy odors warm,
The crimson autumn flowers, that scent
    The airs with perfumed balm,

The sweet cyclamen's dainty blooms,
    The clover's trefoil leaves,
Speak of the summer; but their voice
    But only half deceives.

We know full well 'tis but the lull
    Before the tempest's burst,
These endless, cloudless, lazy days, —
    But why dream of the worst?

A few more days of joy are ours, —
    October's golden days!
More beautiful, more soft, more warm,
    Because of chilly haze

That hangs about their brow at morn,
    Yet flees before the sun,
And gives us back our perfect hours
    'Ere yet the day is done.

Then let us yield ourselves once more
    Unto the magic charm,
That circles all the earth and sky,
    In one long dream of calm.

Then let us feel their love once more
   In this fair, perfect dream;
But let us wander 'mid the woods,
   And by the thread-like stream,

Where wild anemonès, all red
   And purple, deck the flood;
Those vari-colored flowers that sprung,
   Deep in the Cyprian wood;

When Venus, by her lover's side
   Wept his untimely lot,
Dropped nectar o'er his bleeding form,
   These flowers sprang from the spot.

Along the brook, that flows away
   Betwixt the line of hills,
Its volumes fed by gushing springs
   And tiny mountain rills;

Its borders girt with willow trees,
   Like beauties side by side,
They bend their forms to view them in
   The water's mirrored tide.

There let us stray, until we come
   Unto the chestnut wood;
We'll rest beneath its mighty boughs,
   Where shadows gray are strewed;

7

We'll rest and dream away the soft
  And mellow noontide hours;
We'll weave the tall and bearded grass
  With buff cyclamen flowers.

And when the sunset colors burn
  Upon the hills afar,
In splendorous tints of red and gold
  Above the rock's dark bar;

When all the curious, dreamy hue,
  With changing scarlet flush,
Is seen across the summer land,
  Amid the evening's hush,

We'll turn our steps across the meads,
  And greet the swift new-comer, —
We'll greet the dark November days,
  And say good-bye to summer.

THE ROSE-LEAF ON THE WINE.

A sage, from Eastern lands remote,
　To classic Athens came,
Seeking the wisdom he had heard
　Dwelt in that land of fame.

Deep in the city's busy heart,
　A shaded garden stood,
Where learnèd men, — their only love, —
　The ways of wisdom wooed.

In vain he plead his eager cause
　And sought admittance there,
Their answer ever was the same
　To his repeated prayer,

Until at last they wearied grew ;
　So when he came again,
To seek an answer from their lips,
　They sent no word's refrain,

But ushered him in silence, in
   A frescoed chamber dim,
And brought him there a goblet filled
   With red wine to the brim.

" This is our answer!" so they said.
   Straight thro' the sage's mind
There flashed its meaning, as he gazed:
   " No room for more we find;

" Our circle, like the goblet there,
   With members is filled up;
Another drop would prove too much,
   And overflow the cup."

One moment, with the glass in hand
   He paused, until his eye
Fell on a rose that blossomed lone
   Within a vase near by.

He plucked a petal from the flower,
   A rose-leaf pink and fair,
And o'er the goblet's sparkling brim
   He laid it, blushing there.

No drop was spilled; it floated o'er
   The wine's deep mantling tide,
A dainty, fairy, rosy craft,
   Where Puck himself might ride!

A simple thing !   But still it held
  A meaning sweet and rare.
The wise men bade him enter in,
  And make his dwelling there.

A lesson from the rose-leaf take,
  Ye hearts that guard so well
The entrance to the love you hide
  Deep in a prison's cell.

Because you love a favored few,
  Think not your hearts can hold
No other guests ; read o'er the tale
  By ancient sages told.

Think on that goblet, well filled up,
  With rose-leaf o'er the wine.
Pause !   Canst thou in the legend see
  A case that's like to thine ?

THE ETRUSCAN GOLD.

'Twas in Italy; the night was warm
  With the touch of the August days.
I leaned on a marble statue's arm,
  And watched the moonlight's rays,

As they quivered and shimmered along the grass,
  Or fell o'er the olive wood.
The lake's still bosom was smooth as glass.
  'Round the spot, where we silent stood,

Was naught of the present!   But each thing spoke
  Of a past that was half forgot;
As if spirits of men, long dead and gone,
  Yet haunted the lonely spot.

And standing there, in that far-off clime,
  In the soft Italian weather,
I thought of a tale of its early times,
  And strung it in verse together.

'Twas a tale I had heard when a little child, —
    'Twas a tale that was but half-told,
But it all came back as I touched, that night,
    A chain of Etruscan gold,

Woven in thousand filmy threads,
    Plaited fast in a golden rope,
That fell o'er the folds of her soft white dress,
    'Round her warm neck's snowy slope.

The tale was this : In those ages dead,
    Ere were builded the walls of Rome,
In old Etruria's fruitful land,
    The gold-worker made his home.

Those earliest workers in yellow gold,
    Whose art is our art's despair, —
The secret is lost! the magical charm
    That wove all their ornaments rare !

Now there lived in those days, by the city's gate,
    A man, who was poor and alone;
As he sat in the shade of his olive tree
    And listened the cicale's tone,

He wrought in the metal he loved so well,
    With its golden, glimmering sheen ;
It bent to his hand in a fine-drawn line
    That ran the web between, —

Like to the wealth of a maiden's hair,
    That, in many a golden tress,
Falls over her shoulder white and bare,
    With the breath of a soft caress, —

He wove the threads in a thousand forms,
    Till they glistenèd in the sun,
Like the gossamer web we see at morn,
    Which the spider through night has spun.

But he was happy, and loved his life;
    So he wove, thro' the summer long,
The threads of gold, as he sat in the shade
    Murmuring scraps of song.

But alas! for the worker!   There passed one day,
    In the heat of the noon-tide's hour,
On her palfrey white, a princess fair, —
    They called her the " Tuscan Flower!"

She paused in the shade of the olive tree,
    To seek at the wayside well
A cooling draught from its limped depths, —
    Her gaze on the worker fell.

Then she drew her rein and rode away,
    Nor thought of him who stood
And watched her train, as it wound afar
    Through the silvery olive wood.

He turned with a sigh to his art again,
   But his fingers lay idle and still;
He worked no more in the golden threads
   With the touch of his dainty skill.

The olive that stood beside the door,
   Rose 'gainst the sky's pale gold,
And seemed to whisper forever " peace!"
   Then shivered, as if the cold

Had touched it, there on the sun-bathed hill,
   And silenced its spiritual moan ;
But ever amid the night it cried
   " Peace!" in a weary tone.

For there was no " peace " in the worker's heart,
   So the tree, with its emblem sweet,
Dropped ever its mournful, colorless leaves,
   Like tears, at the master's feet.

He would sit and watch the blue mists break
   And drift o'er the land at morn ;
While the clouds, with violet shadows dusk,
   Went over the fresh green corn.

When the tremulous wood-smoke curled on high
   Thro' the waves of the rose-touched air,
And the mountains were flushed like apple-blooms,
   But darkening, here and there,

Where the pine and the cypress, tall and sad,
    Grew purple and dark and dense,
Till the strong, white sun flushed out again
    In fire-opal hues intense.

He would sit and watch, on the far-off hills,
    The olives, like clouds of rain,
Shimmering to silver, with touch of light,
    And murmuring as tho' in pain.

But never his fingers touched the gold!
    They had lost their old-time art!
He wove no more the fine web now,
    For ever across his heart,

There came the shadow of her fair face,
    Then the thread would snap in twain!
All the world grew dark, and his fancy saw
    Her dark eyes flash again!

At last he could bear his grief no more,
    He hungered for but one glance;
So he wandered adown the city's streets,
    Like one in a dreamy trance,

Till he came to her palace grand, that rose
    With its dainty turrets fair;
He slept all night on the marble steps,
    So cold, and white, and bare!

But her servants beat him away with rods,
   Not knowing the love he bore ; —
What right had a beggar, with matted hair,
   To sleep at the palace door ? —

They scourged him with rods, till bruised and torn
   Was the quivering, tender flesh,
And great welts lay like serpents along
   His shoulders, beneath the lash.

He haunted the palace gates no more,
   But out by the city's wall
He dragged himself, till he reached the hut,
   With its olive, white and tall.

But the tree had pined for its master's face ;
   Its leaves were withered and gray,
Like the silver beard of an aged man,
   Who is laid in the tomb away.

Sadly he looked at the " tree of peace ; "
   It shook with the evening wind,
And the leaves that fell at his weary feet,
   Were dead as his peace of mind !

Now it came to pass, as the days went by,
   O'er the land a famine fell ;
In the mournful city was heard all day
   The tones of the funeral bell.

Far over the plains of Tuscany,
   Thro' Umbria's valleys wide,
Where erst the yellow waves of wheat
   And the vines sprung side by side, —

From every valley the prayers arose,
   From every temple grand,
That Bona Dea might look and bless
   The black and barren land.

And lo! the voice of the temple spake:
   " Oh! all ye workers in gold,
Whose fame has spread far thro' the land,
   Your worship has grown too cold!

" If you would atone, I pray you make
   As an offering unto the shrine,
A golden sheaf, and bind it around
   With threads of gossamer fine.

" Spin them all from the yellow gold,
   Twelve thousand threads to adorn,
With their lines all finer than spider's web,
   The golden sheaf of corn!

" Then the land shall blossom all over with blooms;
   Then the blades of the young corn spring;
Then the fields be filled with the harvest rich,
   Where the grilli and cicale ring."

Thus the Oracle spake; and far and wide,
   Through all the desolate land,
The workers in gold tried all in vain
   To answer its hard command.

But each one failed, and failing said:
   "We are men, not gods divine;
Can we spin gold, that the spider's web
   Shall be less frail, less fine?"

They cursed themselves, in their deep despair,
   And cried, "Oh! may we die!
Since we find no mercy upon the earth,
   And none in the bright blue sky!"

Then he, who had loved the "Tuscan Flower,"
   Rose from his wretched state.
Pondering o'er all his ancient skill,
   He cried, "It is not too late!

"Give me of gold, and I will weave,
   In many a fine-drawn line,
Twelve thousand threads that shall be more frail
   Than the web of the spider fine!"

But the people, mocking and sneering, said:
   "A naked, outcast one,
Fleshless of limb and hollow of eye,
   Crawling on under the sun!

" Is it thou that wouldst touch the dainty gold?
    Tempt us not with thy feeble lies!"
They turned on him with strong, fierce words,
    And murder within their eyes!

But still the famine, o'er all the land,
    Spread gristled and gaunt and dark;
By the stony wayside the traveller fell,
    And lay there, rigid and stark!

All day and night, in the city's gates,
    There were swollen and weeping eyes;
The mothers turned their pain-pierced ears
    From their anguished children's cries!

Then the king came down from his weary throne,
    Listening their mournful tale.
He cried aloud, " Give the beggar gold;
    We can be no worse if he fail!"

So they gave him gold, and he shut himself
    In a dreary tower alone,
And wrought till eyes grew heavy and red, —
    Till his heart seemed turned to stone.

Thro' the hours he wrought, 'till he learned again
    The magical, old-time skill;
But the daintest threads he wove at eve,
    When the city was calm and still;

For then in fancy she came again;
   He saw her fair form rise
From the twilight mist, like a spirit come
   From borders of Paradise.

Seven days had passed, when he oped the door,
   Came down from the high, stone tower;
Breathless the million people stood
   In the glare of the noon-tide hour!

And lo! he held within his hand
   Twelve thousand threads of gold!
The people saw, and down their cheeks
   The great tears silent rolled!

It was a scene to make men weep!
   The multitudes that thronged,
With fleshless limbs and hungered eyes,
   The city's streets among!

They followed him with famished gaze
   Unto the temple, where
Upon the steps of marble pure
   The beggar knelt in prayer.

They watched him as he offered up,
   On Bona Dea's shrine,
The thousand threads all spun of gold,
   Than spider's web more fine!

With blood-shot, famished, wolfish eyes
　　They watched!　Deep silence reigned
The temple thro'.　Would she accept?
　　Despairing hopes fast waned!

Then once again the goddess spake, —
　　Her voice was like a flute:
" By gold shall all Etruria live;
　　Let earth bring forth her fruit!"

Quick thro' the parchèd, blackened soil
　　The green blades upward pressed!
Quick ripened into sheaves of wheat,
　　Which were the sweetest, best,

That ever on Etruria's hills,
　　Or in her valleys green,
Were in the merry harvest-time
　　By laughing maidens gleaned!

Then strong the voice of thousands rose:
　　" Upon the king's right hand
Our saviour's place; there's none like him
　　In all Etruria's land!"

But still the beggar lowly knelt
　　Just at the temple's door,
And whispered, " Has it made *her* smile?
　　I ask for nothing more!"

So kneeling there, with outstretched hands,
   While rays of summer sun
Fell gently on the thousand threads
   His loving skill had spun,

He died!   His soul sweet spirits took
   And wafted it to heaven!
For he had proved how much on earth
   For mortal love is given!

But she for whom it all was wrought, —
   She never knew his worth!
Tho' oft her tears of sorrow fell,
   Swift by her laughter's mirth,

When thinking of the one whom death
   Within the temple kissed;
Who dying there, his glories won,
   World's sweetest praises missed!

8

DRIFTING.

Afar upon the golden sands,
   That touch the summer sea,
Some crimson sea-weed joinèd hands
   And drifted merrily,

For days and days, in sweet embrace,
   Along the palm-clad isles
That, in their robes of sheeny green,
   Stretched out for vernal miles.

It drifted on from shore to shore,
   Now seeking happy rest
Upon the top of some high wave,
   With glistening, sunny crest;

And now it played at hide-and-seek
   Upon the liquid blue,
When down the white squall furious came,
   With maddened speed it flew

From wave to wave so merrily,
   In wildest, dancing glee!
What joy to climb the breaker's heights
   Upon the open sea!

Thro' storm and calm it gaily went, —
   A child upon its mother's breast!
So glad the sea-weed gently rocked
   Within its foamy nest.

Now sailing up the crystal creeks
   That dent the sanded shore;
Then floating with the tide again,
   To greet the sea once more, —

O'er dark blue waves, with snow-white manes,
   That move resistless on;
Unchanging, tho' all else may change,
   Thro' endless miles they roam.

It chanced that far upon the wave
   The sea-weed roamed one day,
Far from the sand-begirted shore,
   Amid the waves at play;

Until beside the current warm
   That runs the ocean thro',
The gulf-stream's steady onward flow,
   The joinèd sea-weed drew;

A moment, and their long embrace
    Was severed; one was caught
Within the northward flowing wave;
    The other wildly thought

To follow fast; but, cruel fate!
    There blew an adverse wind,
And powerless to change its course,
    It left its mate behind

And drifted sad and desolate
    O'er many weary miles,
Until it kissed the sands about
    The sunny palm-crowned isles.

There it watched thro' many a year,
    But never came again,
The mate that it had lost that day
    Within the gulf-stream's main.

The one that in the stream was clasped,
    Was ever onward borne,
Until upon the sea-shore here
    At last 'twas idly thrown.

I picked it from the glittering sand,
    On this far Northern shore,
And heard it sigh its sorrow out,
    To see its mate once more. .

How like the joinèd sea-weed are
   Some human lives, alas !
Embraced as if they ne'er would part,
   They drift o'er seas of glass;

They drift upon the summer seas,
   And cool their parchèd lips
Within the dark blue waters, where
   There go the life-built ships.

They drift and dream amid the isles,
   And in the crystal bays ;
They float upon the summer seas
   For many days and days.

And then they venture laughingly,
   Till they unknowing come
Upon the gulf-stream of their lives,
   That bears one far from home,

And casts it on some wild, bleak shore,
   To pine its life away,
And sigh for all the memories
   Of one far, happy day.

The other seeks to follow on,
   Alas ! the sea-weed's fate
Is but an emblem of its own !
   It sees its lovèd mate

By swift relentless currents borne
    Far from its loving clasp ;
It strives to follow, aye, to reach
    That one beyond its grasp !

An adverse wind blows o'er the sea,
    And powerless it goes
Back to those isles, where orange tree
    And flowery myrtle grows,

There still to dream, to dream and wait ;
    But never comes again
The heart it loved ; 'twas lost that day
    Within the gulf-stream's main !

THE ADVENTURES OF CUPID.

One evening, when departing day
With languid grace and beauty lay
Upon the dainty clouds of rose, —
A princess, seeking sweet repose!

And drinking from the silver cup,
With twilight nectar-drops filled up,
Shaped like a silvery birch canoe,
O'erflowing with the sparkling dew. —

Beside a surging inland sea,
Whose wavelets sparkled light and free,
Whose shores were bright with silver sands
And shells that grace the sea-beat strands,

Young Cupid, — dainty, tricksy sprite!
With dancing eyes and spirits light! —
Who often, in a naughtier mood
Than this on which we now intrude,

Hath pierced poor mortals' throbbing hearts
By letting fly his well-aimed darts,
Which, dainty as the god himself,
And like him, too, — the little elf! —

Have mischief as their only aim!
All other ends would seem too tame.
Yes, Cupid, fair but erring child,
By music of the waves beguiled,

And wearied of the gardens fair
Where nymphs to Venus made their prayer,
Had wandered from his Paphian home,
Upon the sea-shore sands to roam.

A nymph, with laughing eyes of blue,
Had teased him till away he flew,
As angry as a child could be!
So first he sought the sandy lea.

So here, far from his mother straying,
Upon the beach we find him playing.
Forgotten now the teasing maid!
He thinks ne'er could he longer stayed

Within his mother's palace grand,
Had he but known of this sweet land,
Where dainty Peris from the waves,
And mermaids from the coral caves,

Disport themselves as merrily
As dryads 'neath the greenwood tree.
Upon the glistening sands he flings
His quiver, while a mermaid sings;

And watch him from his shoulder throw
His mother's gift, his silver bow!
Ah! Cupid, Cupid, much I fear
You'll shed to-morrow many a tear,

For this night's play upon the shore,
While dancing to the ocean's roar!
He leads a Peri in the dance
Till even she one moment pants,

So rapidly he whirls along
Amid the laughing, moving throng!
He sports amid a mermaid's hair,
Which, like a curious winding stair,

Falls down in many a crinkling curl,
With coral woven in, and pearl.
Till came at last the time when they
Must speed to ocean homes away,

To seek the caves where coral grows,
Where beds of sea-weed speak repose.
'Twas now far onward in the night,
And Cupid, left alone, in fright

Crept in a shell, which close at hand
Lay gleaming on the moonlit strand.
Oft, when his mother and her train
Had left their homes upon the plain,

To float awhile o'er ocean's foam,
Afar from Paphos' island home,
Within a sea-shell lined with pearl,
With dainty sails that he could furl,

Young Cupid rested sweet and well;
Nor dreamed that now another shell
Might bring his baby-self to grief!
For ah! his sleep that night was brief!

Unlucky fate! this very shell,
In which the wanderer slept as well
As if on couch of thistle down,
With watching nymphs and graces round,

A monster of the sea possessed, —
A Hermit Crab, that dreadful pest,
Which like the cuckoo steals a home,
And when its rightful owners come,

Will drive them off like pirates bold,
Who think they own whate'er they hold.
When now Aurora's first faint ray
Bespeaks the near approach of day,

The Crab, from journeys, home returns,
And there the little elf discerns.
But tho' he is a thief himself,
He does not care to share his pelf;

He sounds the war-cry loud and long,
Then hastens to avenge his wrong!
Our hero, wakened from his sleep,
From out the shell doth slowly creep.

Alas! poor god! thy fate is sad!
If but one arrow now you had,
You might the foe in battle meet!
Now naught is left but quick retreat!

E'en that, alas! I see, is vain.
The outraged Crab will not disdain
To follow thee with fury wild.
I pity thee, poor erring child!

For onward comes the warrior bold;
Within his claws, so wet and cold,
He clasps the dainty, rosy form,
And tears the skin so white and warm!

The combat wages fierce and fast,
And wounded Cupid sinks at last;
His dainty flesh is scratched and torn,
And golden locks, that once adorned

His little lordship's curly pate,
Have suffered at a dreadful rate ;
His wings are soiled and drooping, too,
And filled with tears his eyes of blue ;

Like fair twin violets, each cup
With drops of summer rain filled up.
Meanwhile within the palace where
Lived Venus and her maidens fair

Sprung frenzy and confusion wild,
For they had missed the truant child ;
And hurrying thro' the wooded grove
They sought the wandering god of Love.

Each sweet nymph vowed to tease no more,
E'en tho' her heart, with arrows sore,
Should testify to Cupid's skill,
When mischief all his soul should fill.

They sought him near, they sought him far ;
While Venus in her pearly car,
Drawn by her snowy milk-white doves,
Whose sweet notes fill the Paphian groves,

Flies onward with the morning wind,
Her darling son resolved to find.
Where, pale and bleeding, Cupid lay,
It happed there sadly came that way,

With weeping eyes, the nymph herself
Who oft had teased the little elf;
She, mourning, begs of gracious heaven
That her past misdeeds be forgiven;

She loudly prays that mighty Jove
Will bring her to the god of Love!
E'en as she speaks, upon the sand,
By perfumed zephyrs sweetly fanned,

She spies the very one she seeks,
And rends the air with wildest shrieks;
Till, hastening o'er the shining sands,
Beside the boy his mother stands,

Her nymphs and graces all around;
Who, now the little wanderer's found,
Are smothering him with kisses sweet.
In piteous tones they still entreat

That he will live for their sweet sakes!
E'en tho' each maiden heart he breaks.
They stanch his wounds with leaves of rose;
They soothe him into sweet repose;

His pains are eased, his curls caressed,
While Venus clasps him to her breast.
They bear him to the pearly car,
And speed with him to groves afar,

Where, round his rose-leaf couch will float,
In measure sweet, the tuneful note
That groves of Paphos know so well, —
The plaintive voice of Philomel!

'Tis thus that Cupid, nursed to life,
Returns again unto the strife;
And with his well-sent arrows move
The hearts of mortals 'gain to love.

Now, fair ones, do you read aright
The story of young Cupid's flight?
When, wearied of your changing fancies,
On others' charms he slily glances,

And leaves you to your jealous fits,
While 'round a rival's bower he flits.
Oh! maidens coy, inconstant ever,
Who torment, tease the faithful lover!

You seek him with a saddened heart;
You love, since drifted far apart;
With wingèd feet and weeping eyes,
You chase young Cupid as he flies;

And ever does he dearer grow,
E'en tho' he smiles at all your woe, —
As oft, in days that now are gone,
You treated him with laughing scorn.

And if unlucky fate befall him,
And woes innumerable enthrall him,
You soothe his sorrow, ease his pain,
And kiss him into life again !

ORIGIN OF THE PEARL.

'Tis said there is a jewel formed
　　By drops of spring-time rain,
That fall in April, from the heavens,
　　Upon the billowy main, —

The " Nisan," tears that Peris weep,
　　When thoughts of Paradise
Bring up the visions they have lost,
　　And fill their souls with sighs, —

These rain-drops fall, so clear and pure,
　　Into the oyster shell,
And soon they bless the hour when they
　　From sky to ocean fell.

For lo ! in place of sparkling drop,
　　A pearl of milky hue !
A virgin in her robes of white
　　Meets now the charmèd view.

Thus, e'en within the saddest life,
  By hard misfortunes spent,
The very tears of grief that fall,
  Like rain from heaven sent,

May sink into the darkened heart,
  And deep within its cell,
Become as precious gem that sleeps
  Within the roughened shell!

Thus many a heart, that doth not wear
  The jewels of the world,
Holds in its secret, spirit depths,
  A pure and priceless pearl!

9

THE ALMA TREE.

There is a tree in Eastern lands,
    Oft sung in Eastern story,
To music of the sweet-toned lute,
    By singers old and hoary.

They tell us of its beauty rare,
    Its sweetest of perfumes,
Of thousand fruits that hang in air
    Beside the thousand blooms.

Thro' all the changing seasons there,
    The Alma tree is laden
With flowers that perfume all the breeze,
    Like winds from distant Aiden, —

That land of beauty and of bloom,
    That happiness reigns over,
Whose flowers and birds and rippling streams
    Would chain the greatest rover!

To-day where falls a flower to earth,
　To-morrow springs another,
And fruits and blossoms ever stand
　As sister unto brother.

So like the ancient Alma tree, —
　A life, where bright hopes ever
Spring by the fruits of deeds sublime
　And buds of strong endeavor.

The seasons change, the years roll on,
　They bring but added honors ;
They bring but flowers and fruits the more
　To shower down upon us.

They bring no wearying of the right,
　No satisfied cessation ;
They bring the fruits of well-spent hours,
　The flowers of consolation !

THE HEART AND THE SHELL.

You wonder why some hearts sing on,
  When all life's coming grace :
And all its beauteous tints are gone,
  And left but sorrow's trace.

I pray thee place this pink sea-shell
  Close, close unto thine ear;
Now tell me, is the music sweet
  Which from its depths you hear?

It sings and sings the livelong day, —
  This dainty, coilèd shell, —
And yet within its polished halls
  No living thing doth dwell.

That which did give it life and breath
  Is left beside the shore,
Where ever on the sanded beach
  The ceaseless waters pour.

'Tis empty now, and yet it sings
    Ever the same strain on,
Because the heart that once beat there
    Is buried now and gone!

And so with human sea-shells borne
    Far from their native shore,
With empty hearts they still sing on
    And echo ocean's roar.

BLACK RUPRECHT.

I mind me, when a little child,
    My nurse would often tell
Of what sad fate a wicked girl
    In olden times befell.

"Black Ruprecht," he who stands without
    The door all thro' the night,
Snatched up this little wicked maid
    And bore her in affright,

Unto his dungeon 'neath the hill,
    Where, far from friends and home,
The erring child was torturèd
    By many a fiendish gnome.

And so when I, rebellious grown,
    Showed angered wilful ways,
My nurse, with many a menace given,
    Aloud her voice would raise,

And cry, "Black Ruprecht is without ;
　　I hear him at the door !
Now cease your cries, or he will come
　　With his black horses four,

"And bear you to his dungeon deep.
　　Hark !　Even now I hear
His footsteps all around the house ! "
　　My heart stood still with fear !

All anger in my heart was stilled ;
　　In trembling tones I asked
That Ruprecht might not bear me off ;
　　Then quickly learned my task.

But now to woman's years I've grown, —
　　No nurse to scold me more,
To threaten me with shrillest tone,
　　"Black Ruprecht's at the door ! "

And yet whene'er my heart is filled
　　With anger, pride, and hate,
It seems to me there vengeful stands
　　Some sorrow at the gate !

Some sorrow deep, that soon will stem
　　My wicked passion's tide,
And teach me, tho' I see him not,
　　" Black Ruprecht " waits beside !

DREAMING.

I roved one day, far, far away
In that sweet wood, where ever play
The birds and bees among the trees,
Each moving, with the moving breeze.

Far from the town I sat me down ;
Far from the world's cold, chilling frown,
And dreaming past the hours fast, —
The happy hours that could not last !

Above me hung, the boughs among,
A mocking-bird, who sweetly sung,
And lulled to sleep, with music deep,
The eyes that were so used to weep !

I lay across a bank of moss,
All fringed with ferns as fine as floss ;
The maiden's hair grew richly there,
As if indeed, a maiden rare

Had thrown her locks across the rocks,
To shield them from all outward shocks ;
The trembling fern my eye discerned,
All quivering, as it's heart did yearn

For one afar, perhaps the star
That follows Dian's silvery car!
In mossy bank my footfall sank,
And where the reeds grew rich and rank.

My bended arm, so white and warm,
Was nestling 'mid the vernal charm
Of violets and wind-flowers set,
To make a flowery tinted net,

Thus to ensnare the bees who dare
To rest within those precincts fair.
The canopy of clear blue sky
Was hidden by the tree-tops high ;

But still anon, from out the sun,
A straggling ray came dancing down ;
Yes, down it came, the straying flame,
And kissed the wind-flowers into shame !

Near by my lip, the cooling drip
Of waters I could easy sip,
Flowed gently down, where lay the town,
In sun of summer, bare and brown ;

Yes, gently by, with half a sigh,
That it might there forever lie
And dream away, from day to day,
Existence in one endless play!

Yet still it flows, still onward goes
'Twixt banks where bloom the sweet wild rose;
'Twixt narrow banks, where serried ranks
Of marshy canes the water flanks.

In this lone spot, by man forgot,
I dreamed away the noontide hot;
I lay and dreamed, and half-way deemed,
'Twere best to be a woodland stream,

That singeth low, when soft winds blow;
And when there comes the winter's woe,
In icy bands, so patient stands,
Nor sighs to seek the summer strands;

That it were best, to seek the rest
Of hearts all sore with crucial test,
Within the wood, beside the flood,
As once of old did Robin Hood!

Thus dreaming on, my thoughts would run,
While evermore the evening sun
Played o'er my face with dainty grace,
Or seemed to run a merry race

With limpid tide, that, dimpling wide,
Ran down my little nook beside.
Tho' storms may fret, I'll ne'er forget
That dainty spot, so quaintly set

In woodland heart, far, far apart
From din and clangor of the mart;
The silver stream, that like a dream,
Ran gladly on, with threadlike gleam;

The mossy seat, where green ferns meet
Above the head, around the feet;
The little nest, where thickly rest
The violets with purple breast;

The birds that sing, or droop the wing,
Beside that little woodland spring; —
All these have power unto this hour!
Again I smell the violet flower!

Again I hear, now far, now near,
The falling of the brooklet's tear!
Again I see the yellow bee, —
The pirate of the flowery sea, —

Go circling round, then sinking down
Deep in the heart where honey's found!
Oh! would that I again might fly
Unto that spot! Once more I'd try

My soul to steep in dreamings deep,
Nor turn away my eyes to weep.
But fate denies those tender ties;
My lot is cast 'neath other skies!

HE SINGS BECAUSE HE CAN BUT SING.

He sings because he can but sing, —
 This is the poet's line;
This beaker holds for his pure lips
 The sweetest of the wine.
He sings because he can but sing,
And beauty finds in every thing.

He sings because he can but sing;
 No priest of art is he,
To sing but for the love of gold,
 Or immortality!
And if his voice doth make sad moans,
It echoes but his spirit tones.

He sings because he can but sing;
 The words *will* upward swell,
And if he force them roughly back,
 He sounds their funeral knell!
So still he gives them leave to spring,
And sings because he can but sing!

The nightingale within the wood,
  Hath sweetest music note;
He sings because he cannot keep
  The music in his throat; —
'Tis not for glory he doth wake
The echoes of the hill and lake!

He cannot choose but utter, in
  Those music-compelling lays,
The songs that gather in his heart
  Thro' all the summer days.
Were he to sing for glistening gold,
His song, to me, would soon grow cold.

Whene'er his heart is sorrowful,
  His music groweth sad;
And yet the song to me is dear
  As when his tones were glad;
Because it cometh from the heart, —
Is of his very life a part!

Then, when the wings of sorrow touch
  The sweet-tongued singer's soul,
Must he, unnatural, quell the voice
  With reason's stern control?
Ah! no; tho' sorrowful they ring,
He sings because he can but sing!

He sings because he can but sing;
  No reason's power is his,

To crush to earth his rosy dreams
  Or grey-cowled memories.
He sings, nor knows the reason why, —
Gives smile for smile, and sigh for sigh!

THE DIFFERENCE.

Some hearts are like the violet's purple flower, —
    They hide their sweetness deep from common
        gaze;
But he who knows their secret dwelling-place,
    From dusty high-road far, 'mid wooded ways, —

May seek and find within their perfumed hearts
    The faint, sweet odors that are hidden there,
And breathing them, contented is to rest,
    Rich in the gift of their pure beauties rare.

And some are like the royal-robèd rose,
    That sheds its perfume to the wanton wind;
No need to ask, for it will freely give;
    Yet in its breast deep treasures still we find.

And some are like the strange Ixora flower,
    That, rich in coloring, heavy with perfume,
Exhales its sweetness in a single hour,
    And in its glory hurries towards the tomb.

And some hearts barren are, like to those leaves
  Which, when they are growing, yield no sweet-
      ness up;
But crush and bruise them, they are odorous
  As e'en the violet, with its dark-blue cup.

Some lives there are that thro' long years have
  grown,
  'Mid all the glories of God's summer light,
And given naught. To them sudden comes
  A crushing sorrow in the darkened night;

All bruised and bleeding, like the scentless leaf,
  From high estate the poor life fallen lies!
But lo! it sets its garnered sweetness free!
  From out the dust its odorous perfumes rise!

10

TO THE BUTTERFLIES.

Gay butterflies, aerial flowers,
　　Who dart among the roses,
Say, do you go, in summer hours,
　　Where my sweet love reposes?

Like flying leaves of autumn days,
　　In gold and blue and yellow,
With here and there some crimson rays,
　　As thro' the air you follow!

Blue butterflies, deep azure dyes
　　Your wings of thistle-down;
You stole your colors from the skies,
Or from the violet of her eyes,
　　With dark lash curled around;

So circled are your azure sails
　　With soft, black velvet rings;
So curling lash, her blue eye veils,
　　Dark as those on your wings.

Oh! butterflies of yellow tint,
  No other shade upon you,
So is her hair's gay, golden glint,
  Its glories far beyon' you!

Ye crimson ones, who take your hues
  From scarlet pomegranate flower,
Take care, lest ye your beauty lose
  Upon her lip's red dower!

And ye who seem like snowy flake
  Upon the ether blue,
Who float far o'er the aerial lake
  In a barque of a drop of dew;

Ye ones that go like drifts of snow, —
  Now swift, now slow, now high, now low,
Where soft winds sigh, where rough winds
    blow, —
Ye are no whiter than her brow
  Ye butterflies of snow!

Gay butterflies that sink and rise,
  Deep in the dewy dell;
Together dart, then float apart, —
Fly on, fair ones, to my sweetheart! —
  Fly from your lily-bell!

On, on, ye pure, ye snow-white blooms,
  Ye breathing flowers of air!

On, on, nor rest until you reach her,
  And crown her wealth of hair

With black and scarlet, blue and gold,
  How many a sparkling gem !
A crown of diamonds would seem dull
  Beside this diadem !

Then onward go, sweet butterflies,
  And rest around her pillow,
Where, half-way dreaming, sweet she lies,
  On moss-bed 'neath the willow.

THE MUSIC OF THE HEART.

It seems a little thing, indeed, —
   The music of the heart;
With all our noisy, changing life
   And it so far apart!

It seems a little thing, indeed,
   To wake the music's tone,
And yet its chords responsive thrill
   To but one touch alone!

And tho' it seems so small a thing
   To set the music free,
And press with tender fingers on
   The joy or sorrow key;

Yet to arouse those silent notes,
   In melodies of song, —
To touch the heart 'till it shall be
   Yet braver and more strong, —

Is e'en a deed that would repay
 A lifetime spent in art ;—
To know the chords of music strung
 Within the human heart !

IN ZULULAND.

Hemmed in on every curving side
  By Zulu's savage hordes,
Resolving there to fight or fall,
  Some British soldiers stood.

Quick from the shadows of the kraal,
  And from the matted grass
That hid their naked, dusky forms,
  Amid its thick morass,

The wily savage lithely rose,
  Came headlong, spear in hand,
And rushed with blood-thirst fury on
  The small, but gallant band!

Pierced through with spears of assegais,
  The brave men swiftly fell;
But not till they had crushing sent
  An awful burst of shell,

Amid the Zulu's thickened ranks,
  That swift, relentless ploughed,
And hid the English from their gaze
  As with a heavy cloud!

But those brave soldiers know too well
  The fate that for them lies;
That soon their eyes will close, to wake
  Again in Paradise!

With swift-drawn breath, a soldier turns
  To one who stands beside;
That one is but a twelve-year boy,
  His father's life and pride!

The warrior's eyes grow dark and dim,
  His breath comes hard and fast,
He clasps his arms around his boy,
  And feels it is the last!

A saddled steed stands waiting by;
  He flings the boy's lithe form
Upon its back; his lips are touched
  With one kiss, long and warm!

Then choking down the rising tear,
  In husky voice he cried,
" Fly for your life, and tell to her
  How well your father died!"

He loosed the rein, and pointed down
    A path that yet was free;
Then flashed like fire the boy's dark eye!
    No braver lad than he!

From out the saddle swift he sprung,
    And laid the stinging lash
Across the steed; it maddened, reared,
    Then flew like lightning's flash!

"My father, I will die with you!"
    No other word was said,
For swiftly to the place they held,
    O'er bleeding British dead,

The Zulus came, with horrid yell
    And hands all crimson-dyed;
That father brave and noble son,
    The awful hordes defied!

Within the boy's small, sun-burned hand
    A flashing pistol gleamed;
He did not tremble, tho' he stood
    Where waves of crimson streamed!

One moment! And the Zulus rushed
    On father and on son!
And surging back! oh God! you saw
    That there was left but one!

Upon his knee the soldier fell,
  Beside his dying boy,
And caught his last low-murmured words,
  " To die here !   Oh! what joy !"

Before his keen, unerring aim
  Five cruel demons fell,
And then he sank beside his son !
  And English soldiers tell,

How side by side the brave pair lay,
  As tho' each spirit saith :
" We loved each other best in life,
  Divide us not in death !"

THE SINGER'S FATHERLAND.

A poet, who had drunk the cup
Of sorrow's bitter wine filled up,
Whose noble soul had sickened been
Of world's frivolity and sin,
With aimless steps had come afar
From out the city's great bazaar.

At eventide he wandered in
A forest dim, when the sun did 'gin
To pale its rays, where light had been,
   And sat him down
Beside a fountain fair to see,
Whose waters sparkled merrily,
And chased each other, as in glee,
   Around and round.

Above him, oaks of ancient day, —
Fit temples for the Druid's lay, —
Were casting shadows o'er the way,
   And rearing high

Their sun-kissed heads, as if in pride,
To look upon the world so wide,
To stand there always, side by side,
  Outlined against the sky !

Each bough, bedecked with glossy leaves,
A canopy of emerald weaves,
While sunlight streams, like golden sheaves,
  The cracks between ;
And bough and limbs all interlace,
To form a lovely sylvan place
And background for the poet's face,
  Who there is seen.

The turf beneath is soft and green,
As costly piles of velveteen
  Bedecking beauty's home ;
And lovely enough to be
The home of sylvan sprite so free,
That in these woods right joyfully
  Might often roam.

The dainty, tiny cups of moss
Would seem as goblets, — none too gross
  To serve a fairy band ;
While the drops of dew they often hold
Are drunk by fays, as once of old,
The gods drank from their cups of gold
  The nectar grand.

Unto this place, by nature blest,
There came, to drink from nature's breast,
One of her children, loved not best,
   But very dear, —
The poet of the thoughtful brow,
Who dwell'st not on what is now,
   But what is yet to be.

His mind was filled with noble things,
But his fantasy had found no wings;
He thought it vain to tune the strings
   That touched the world, —
To make the pulse of nations beat
In fever throb, with fever heat,
   And bear unfurled
This singer's name on fame's bright scroll;
That o'er the wave his fame should roll,
And bless with praise his poet's soul.

His eyes were deep and fathomless,
And peering in them, one might guess
   How god-like was his mind!
And gazing on his saddened face,
You felt as if you saw the trace
   Of things that were behind.

A smile so sweet now hovered there,
That one might think, unseen in air,
The wings of angels bright and fair
Had left their shadowy radiance there!

The poet lay, with idle grace,
On velvet mould at oak tree's base,
And in low voice began to trace
  The thoughts within his mind;
That were to him, in present mood,
Both spirit-drink and spirit-food,
That stirred him up for future good,
  To serve mankind.

His thoughts ran on, like idle hours
We've spent in May among the flowers;
And lying there, he wove in song,
A question he had puzzled long.

"Oh, Muse of the harp and sounding shell,
Whose sweet low tones we know so well,
Whose voice is like a silver bell,
Who dwellest alone in ferny dell,
I pray thee write, with thy white hand,
Upon the golden, sunlit strand,
Where is the Singer's Fatherland?"

He stood and waited for it long;
He wooed the air with festive song;
His heart was hopeful then and strong;
He had asked of many, 'mid the throng,
Where is the Singer's Fatherland?"

Then, noiseless as the sun's bright ray
From heaven's throne, at break of day,

Comes to the earth in sunny May,
And lights the morn's fast fading gray,
So, noiseless, came a lonely band
Of spirit minstrels on every hand,
From out their distant fatherland!

With hoary locks, well touched by time;
With long, white beards, like snowy rime;
With sad, dark eyes that outward peer;
With hearts that never knew a fear;
    They then stood forth, —
    The noble minstrels of the North!

From Norway's snow-encircled clime,
The very cradle-place of rhyme,
They sang of gods of ancient time;
Of mighty deeds that Odin wrought;
Of battles that brave Thor had fought;
Of powers of darkness set at naught
    By Scandinavia's warlike gods.

A woven crown of Norway pine,
Beset with frozen dew-drops fine,
Crowned now the snow-haired minstrel nine.
They touched their harps with trembling hand,
And answered, " On Valhalla's strand
There *is* the Singer's Fatherland!"

They, sighing, ceased.   And then uprose
The bard of Scotia's joys and woes, —

The great Sir Walter; he whose pen
Loved well the portraits of warlike men,
But *best* each Scottish moor and fen!

Beside him stood, in "hodden gray,"
The Peasant Poet; in his day
He charmed the world with simple lay ; —

"Puir Robbie Burns," with song as sweet
As that daisy crushed beneath his feet ;
Whose life, like that "crimson-tippèd flower,"
Had early death for its earthly dower!

They smiling answered, while they wound
A silver thistle and heather crown,
"The Fatherland can here be found!"

With oval face and eyes that smile,
As holding secrets all the while,
From out the shadows comes Nature's child,

The Bard of Avon, by Stratford town ;
Whose name shall roll with mighty sound,
The cycle of coming ages down!

Sweet Avon! in his verse we see
Thy banks of thyme and grassy lea,
And waters flowing to the sea.

Not 'neath Westminster's vaulted dome
Does the poet rest in his last, long home,

But by the sweet banks of his own loved river,
Where the field-birds sing and the sun-rays
     quiver,
He sleeps the sleep of the dead forever!

Then after him, in mystic train,
There followed fast, as drops of rain
Quick pattering on the window-pane,
The characters his pen had wrought
From out the shadowy realms of thought.

Here sad-eyed Lear and Egypt's queen
Stood side by side, in regal mien;
And grim old Shylock, like a fiend;
And Desdemona's pale, sad face,
By the swarthy Moor, of a passionate race.

These creatures of his brain were there,
To wreathe his aureole of hair
With the bay, the laurel, and myrtle fair;
And England's banner to unfurl
And crown him poet of the world!

With sightless eyes upraised to God
Blind Milton stood. He kissed the rod,
And kissing, raised his soul to God!

And Byron, who was wont to cull
Sweet nuts, yet chose the bitter hull,
And poison found in the beautiful!

He steeped himself in wickedness, —
For crime, he thought, was fathomless.
Like the fiery dart of a serpent's tongue,
His words his enemies have stung;
And yet those words his own soul wrung,
Till like the serpent, of which we've read,
He drove his fangs in himself instead,
And in the land of the Greek lay dead!

What say these poets of Albion's strand,
With their locks tossed wild, in the sea-breeze
        fanned?
" Here, here is the Singer's Fatherland!"

His curls entwined with the shamrock wild,
Steps forth the poet of Erin's isle,

And claims that there, on the Irish lake
Whence the famous songs of Killarney wake,
And nature showers her gifts to make
    On earth an Eden fair,
Was first the home where poets sung,
And first the place where loudly rung
Those tones of music, which were strung
    To chords that are most rare.

But not to thee, oh Emerald Gem
In Ocean's sparkling diadem,
Can we award the laurel crown,
To bind thy fair young brows around,

Or say, upon thy sea-beat strand
Is the Singer's first, best Fatherland!

Impatient, dark-eyed sons of France,
Arouse ye now and wield the lance,
To prove your land of song and dance
   Was first the Singer's home ;
That on her sloping, vine-clad hills,
Beset with merry, laughing rills,
   Nature's true poets roam !

Thy poets, wits, are famed and keen, —
Thy sad Corneille, and gay Racine,
And patriotic Lamartine,
   Will still enhance
The glory of thy ancient name,
And rescue thee from every shame,
   Oh ! fair, yet fallen France !

E'en now, from o'er your sacred dust,
You raise your eyes, with hope and trust
   That yet the Fleur-de-Lis
May lift its golden head once more,
Amid the battle's din and roar,
   And Alsace 'gain be free !

What singer cometh from the Rhine
To pay his court at Poet's shrine ?
Has Germany no poet grand
To chant the praises of her land ?

Here Goethe comes, with soul sublime,
To flash, like lightning, from clime to clime,
And strive to burst the bonds of time!
He sought to rise from mortal things, —
To soar aloft on spirit-wings.
His soul was more than usual growth;
To die in God he was not loath.

Schiller and Goethe; there they stand, —
Twin-brother poets of one same land, —
In voices musical and deep
They sing, " It is our own to keep
The honored soil where poesie
In her own resting-place may be."

But who comes here in ancient guise?
Oh! poets of every land, arise
And shout your anthems to the skies!
Stretch forth the hand of fellowship to Italy!
E'en Shakespeare's self would bend the knee
To that fair land of poetry!

Its very skies are deeper blue
Than e'er in other lands you knew;
Its mountain peaks more purple far
Than the royal-hearted pansies are;
Its bays have whiter crested waves
Than the arms of the nymph who in them laves;
Its valleys such bright emerald,
That e'en the gem itself seems dull.

With its handsome men, and its maidens' eyes,
Innocent as doves, yet serpent-wise,
It is on earth a Paradise!

What wonder that such land could give
Sweet poets, through all time to live!
Enthroned and bowered in classic shades,
Virgil, whose glory never fades;
Dante, with face as dark and stern
As those who in his Inferno burn, —
And yet, as lover, he did earn
   The smiles of Beatrice;
And Petrarch, whose poetic lyre
Would ne'er been touched but for love's fire,
That swept its chords and brought him nigher
   To heaven, in Laura's kiss.

Last, Tasso; all his fame entwined
With Leonora's name. His mind,
E'en when half-crazed, could find
In all things beautiful but one, —
Leonora's face was Tasso's sun!

Italia's poets have ever sung
Woman's praises; their verse has rung
With her sweet name, and always flung
   Around her beauty's veil.
A woman, then, would sure award
To them the crown, with gems bestarred,
Knowing full well that they will guard
   It ever, without fail.

Then minstrels sweet, from every clime,
Whose songs are sung throughout all time,
  Come now, draw near,
And tribute pay to poetry,
In her dear land, fair Italy!

The minstrels of the North bend low
Their heads, besprinkled with the snow,
  And offer up
Their crowns of pine from Norway hills,
And feast their eyes, as one who fills
With water from the mountain rills
  His drinking-cup.

The silver thistles and bright blue-bells,
With heather from the Scottish fells,
  Are laid in tribute there;
And England's roses, red and white,
That years agone led on the fight
  'Tween York and Lancaster;

While fresh as on its native rock
There blooms the graceful, green shamrock,
  To Erin ever dear.

And clinging tendrils of the vine,
Brought from the hills beyond the Rhine,
To wreathe around the poet's shrine,
  Like memories green,
That round sad lives do interlace,

And deftly hide each sorrow's trace
  With glistening sheen.

And last, its graceful head bent down,
As if to shield from any wound
  Of foreign spear or lance,
The golden-hearted Fleur-de-Lis,
That once, supreme on land and sea,
  Was called the flower of France.

Then, like a grand old organ's roll,
There rose this anthem from every soul,
" In Italy, oh! minstrel band,
  There is the Singer's Fatherland ! "

THE MOCKING-BIRD.

Within the depths of vernal, leafèd wood,
   Close by the lapses of the summer sea,
A house, all weather-stained and darkened, stood,
   Hemmed in by heights of towering live-oak tree, —

That locked their limbs in many a strong embrace,
Wound in and out; again did interlace,
And shadows threw o'er all the lonely place, —

An old-time Southern home; it still doth stand,
An emblem of our blasted, shattered land.

It chanced that fate did bring my steps one day
   Unto that mansion old,
And tired and worn with all the weary way,
   I made me bold
To seek one night of rest,
Within the quaint, oak-shadowed nest.

The wish was granted; soon the night came on;
I laid me down to dreams of memory born.

Thro' the rough casement, stealing like a thief,
   Came gently and unseen the soft sea-breeze,
That wandering far from off some coral-reef,
   Thro' odorous pines and gnarlèd forest-trees,
Did touch my face, and whisper in the gloom
    A thousand fancies sweet,
    Of sea-waves' sounding beat
    By some sad shore's retreat;
Its music rose and fell thro' all the room!

And then the pungent breath from out the pine-tree
      cones,
And like a sad nocturne, the faint, sweet moans,
   That rock themselves to sleep,
   To the music strong and deep
That ever dwells within the forest's tones.

High in the southern sky the yellow moon,
   Half veiled in robes of mist, —
As when Artemis, on old Latmos' mount,
   The fair Endymion kissed, —
Sped on her course, the azure fields among;
The music of the spheres right sweetly rung
   About her flying feet,
   Well sandallèd and fleet,
As when from Alpheus they fled,
Until the skin, thorn-piercèd, bled,

And roses red sprang from the blood,
And blossomed in the spring-time wood.

And ever and anon a ray came dancing down;
Far through the ether blue
With lightsome speed it flew!

Twixt oak boughs, rich with dark green beryl,
It fell, in streams of liquid pearl,
      Across the floor,
        Thro' all the room,
      And glimmered, glowing
        Thro' the gloom.

As there I lay, my soul half mersed
   In dreams of memory,
Across my listening ear came first
   A note of minstrelsy,
So sweet, and yet withal so sad,
   I knew not why it made me glad.

I listened! once again it came,
   So long, so sweet, so clear!
   No music I shall ever hear
   Will come again so very near
My inmost heart!   Again it came,

But nearer, clearer than before,
As if the bird would then outpour
In song its boundless music's store;

Until it loosed, nay, wildly tore
   The heavenly song from out its throat,
   That it might upward gently float,
   And fall, each throbbing, swelling note,
Down at the heavenly door,
   That guards the entrance to the skies,
   Where dwells the holy and the wise !

Another voice takes up the song
In answer clear, but not so strong ;
And as the notes flow swift along,
   The live-oaks fairly seem to bend,
     As 'twere with most exquisite pain,
   To hear the mock-birds in their boughs,
     Unite in such a heavenly strain.

The flood of music swells and falls,
As tho' it brake 'gainst crystal walls
Which shattered it, and sent it back,
Far down the blue and silver track
That it had climbed to reach the stars,
Firm set in gold and azure bars !

Till once again it rose and fell,
As dropping down a crystal well.
It swells and falls so wild and free
In one unbroken symphony,
Like some forgotten memory,
   That in a moment breaks upon
     The heart that had forgot,

And bringeth back, with sweetest pain,
Some dear, remembered spot.

It swells, and falls, and quivers long;
It trilleth in sweet rills of song,
That run your throbbing veins along,
     In laughing rills
     That madly thrills,
     And wildly fills
     The echoes of the echoing hills!

Till fainter, fainter, far away,
It sadly, sweetly, seems to say,
"I cannot stay, I cannot stay."

List to that last sweet fairy note!
Ah! far away I hear it float!
Be still! my throbbing, surging heart!

     Still, still, I hear!
     Upon mine ear
     It faints, it dies,
     Against the skies;
     It strives to rise,
     Then faintly dies
     Against the skies!

But what is that? E'en as it dies,
Far in the hollow of the skies;
When on my ear, I think I hear
The last, sweet, lingering note,

Again there bursts, as did at first,
   A surging, throbbing melody,
Of wildest, maddest minstrelsy,
   Of glorious, wild-note harmony!

It rocketh like a rocking boat
   Upon the dancing tide,
Until the listening ear is drunk
   And dizzy with its glide.

It quivering dwells, as if it spells
   Were quickly coming after,
And then it breaks in flumes and flakes
   Of sweetest song-bird laughter,

That seem to fairly touch and shake
The very highest rafter
Of that blue-archèd, moon-lit dome,
Which is the soaring sky-lark's home!

I listen, soundless silence falls
All thro' the oaken-bowered halls.
Where has the tinkling laughter fled?
   So short it stopped, the note
Must somewhere be; and e'en if dead,
   'Twould round me float!

     When fainting died, the stars beside,
       That last unearthly strain,
     I almost knew the note so true
       Would come again!

But why so sudden cease?
  It were not best
To rob me of my peace
  With sweet unrest.

For now my strainèd ear,
  Uncloyed with sweet,
Its longing all unsatisfied,
  With blisses fleet,

Doth listening wait;
  The silence gives it pain.
Oh! saddest fate!
  Will it ne'er come again?—

Oh! what sweet melody
  Fills all the air,
Falling like jewels rich
  Down a golden stair;

Rising in fair harmonies
  To the gracious skies;
Rising sweet, swift to greet
  Souls in Paradise!

Thro' the earth, thro' the air,
  Far up in the heaven,
Floats out the sweetest song
  Ever to bird given.

Sing on, sweet mocking-bird,
  Carolling to thy mate,
Listening to thy heavenly strain,
  I'd bar the gates to hate
And open wide the doors of love,
And soar with thee the earth above !

Thou brief epitome of song,
For whose sweet notes my soul would long
    In Paradise ;
Sing on, sweet bird, sing on,
Nor cease thy song till dawn
    Doth touch the skies !

.

FATE.

Where'er the flowers are
  The butterflies come too ;
With bright-hued golden wings,
  The fair queen rose to woo.

Where'er the sweet grapes hang
  Are murmuring crowds of bees, —
The bold free-lancers of the fields,
  In swarms of two and threes.

Where'er the lovers whisper,
  The burning fire-flies come,
As if they knew on lover's lips
  Was first their glowing home.

Where coral honeysuckle grows
  The humming-bird darts in,
For well he knows the sweets that dwell
  The chaliced cup within.

FATE.

Where'er the grasses spring,
　　The soft, sweet south winds hover,
With breathless bliss, they kiss
　　The fields of summer clover.

Thus each fair child of nature
　　Hath for its heart a mate ;
Deny not, then, my tender thoughts, —
　　Since loving is but fate !

THE KING IS DEAD!

"The King is dead! Long live the King!"
This is the fickle song we sing;
The stroke that tolled the Old Year's death
Gave to the New Year life and breath.

"The King is dead!" We bring no flower
To deck his tomb at midnight hour;
We shed but tears to his memory dear,
And bid "good-by" to the sad "Old Year."

Last night, when ceased the city's hum,
And the mystic hour of twelve had come,
The year that came to us bright and fair
Was laid in its grave, so dark and drear.

'Twas ushered in with prospects sweet, —
A nation's hopes lay at its feet;
Those hopes are crushed, the year is dead, —
The spirit of '77 has fled!

Drop on its coffin, one by one,
The months that have so quickly gone ;
Slowly and sadly count them o'er,
While the New Year stands at the open door.

'Twas a year of change — a year of blood, —
And dark misfortunes, like a flood,
Swept swift across our broad, fair land,
From the ocean's shore to the Rio Grande.

In Washington, 'neath the marble dome
Where Liberty erst had her home,
" Fraud " spread her banner to the world,
And Liberty to earth was hurled.

When Summer smiled upon the plain,
And Nature sung one glad refrain,
There came from crowded cities far,
The awful din and sound of war.

A war between the rich and poor ; —
God grant the New Year hold no store
Of this, the saddest strife of strife,
When brother seeks a brother's life.

'Twas a sweet "Old Year" to many a heart, —
A year from which 'twas sad to part ;
But it's day is past, " farewell " is said,
And sadly we whisper, " the King is dead ! "

"Long live the king" is the joyous song
Of every heart in the merry throng
Of those who come their court to pay
To '78 on New Year's Day.

It brings to us a vista fair,
Of lovely "castles in the air,"
May its dreams and hopes fulfillèd be,
Whene'er "our ship comes home from sea!"

LAYS OF THE REPUBLIC.

When wandering on the wave-kissed shores
   Of the land of fame, the Grecian isles,
Blind Homer touched his lyre and sung
   Of Paris' love, of Helen's wiles:

He sought the aid of Clio, muse
   Of history, glory, and renown;
That he might tell, in fiery words,
   Of Priam's fate, of Ilium's town.

In this fair Western land of ours,
   Afar from Tempe's lovely vale,
With no Pierian spring to taste,
   No lofty Helicon to scale,

I'll not invoke the muse's aid;
   Let Greece her every romance keep,
Her's is a beauty that is dead;
   In their marble tombs her heroes sleep.

But our fair land is a land of life,
    Its tale of triumph, an epic grand;
Its heroes' names enrolled have been,
    Upon the scroll in Fame's right hand.

Their bold deeds then my theme shall be,
    The hallowed spots baptized in gore,
That make us feel the fiery blood,
    Which burned in Texans' veins of yore.

As a pilgrim who visits the shrine of his saint,
    To thee, San Antonio, I've come;
To feast mine eyes on thy beauty quaint,
    To wander thy streets among.

As drank the novice of ancient days
    From the fabled well of the muses nine,
So do I drink from the limpid waves,
    That sparkle like golden wine.

Thus runs, 'tis said, an ancient legend, —
    A line in an old-time Spanish strain, —
That " whoso drinketh thy waters once,
    Oh! San Antonio, shall drink again."

Do they still possess the magical spell,
    The fairy-like power to bring
From afar the wanderer weary,
    Who once hath drunk at their spring?

Then drink I again San Antonio,
  'Tis a draught of enchantment I'm sure;
May it serve in the future my wandering steps
  Near thy bloom-bordered banks to allure.

Inspire me, thou loveliest of rivers!
  A veil o'er thee Romance doth fling;
Then rend it and tell me thy story,
  That I of thy heroes may sing.

'Twas years ago that a ventursome band,
  From their homes mid the hills of Spain,
Came searching for gold and for treasure,
  To this, our fair land of the plain.

De Soto and his few brave followers;
  Then La Salle and his daring men,
De Leon and gallant St. Denis,
  Whose names history's watchwords have been.

As the years rolled on, there often came,
  From the lands beyond Mississippi's waters,
Bands of settlers brave and strong,
  To win sweet homes for sons and daughters.

They made then a home in the wild wood;
  They fought with the Indian foe,
That roamed from the far red waters
  To the Rio Grande's flow.

But war's dark cloud now settled o'er
  The skies that erst were only fair,
And despotism's galling yoke
  Has roused the lion from his lair !

In Mexico, that city grand,
  Of towering dome and marble wall,
That once, a poet gazing on,
  "The Venice of the Aztec" called;

Santa Anna holds his court supreme,
  Built on the wreck of Freedom's tower;
"Republican," no longer now
  Can be the boast, the well-earned dower

Of Texas men, unless they rise
  And free them from the Mexican chain;
If listless, supine, now they lie,
  The brightness of their star will wane.

Its glory dimmed, to rest 'twill sink
  In blackness deep as shrouds the grave,
With not one line its fate to tell,
  Unless it be the word of "slave."

Think not because their guise was rough,
  Their hearts beat not as warm and true
As soldiers who, at Marathon,
  The Persian hosts in triumph slew.

Tho' few in numbers, they did bring
   To aid their cause a purpose great;
When men like these resolve to do,
   They are themselves their only fate;

Their spirits brave could not endure
   To feel the tyrant's heavy thrall.
With them 'twas " Liberty or death ;"
   They proved their creed at freedom's call !

In the days of bright October,
   When the wild grape purple grew,
From our city by the seashore
   To San Antone the good news flew,

That resistance strong and armed
   Should be meted to the foe ;
That no more Santa Anna's minions
   Would have power for weal or woe.

Lingering long in Mexic dungeons,
   Where no rays of sunlight came,
Austin, from dark prisons freed,
   Came to kindle into flame

The fires of hope, of freedom bright,
   That, burning in the hearts of men
Have empires, kingdoms overturned ;
   This they have done, shall do again !

O'er the land the tidings flew,
  Every heart its anthem echoed, —
From the coast by waters blue,
  To the south by rivers checkered.

From the banks of Arkakisa, —
  Trinity, we now doth name, —
Come the sound of many voices,
  Voices then unknown to fame.

From the shady banks of Nueces,
  From the Brazos, Tockauhono,
Cibolo and Medina bright,
  Clear Colorado, Pashohono.

Louder yet the strain is ringing,
  " Come brave hearts and glory win ! "
From San Jacinto, Guadalupe,
  And Navidad they gather in !

Gonzales, by the Guadalupe,
  The Lexington of Texas is ;
There first the cannon's roar proclaimed
  Her liberty ; a place it is,

Endeared to every Texan heart,
  With ties as strong as those which bind
The Briton to fair Runnymede,
  Or German to the towered Rhine.

Now comes in truth the shock of war, —
 A war where men of sternest mould
Lead the assault, and still urge on
 Their followers with accents bold;

Till cold in death the hand that once
 Did beckon on, where showed the breach,
And stilled the voice that often stirred
 Their souls sweet victory to reach.

It was night, the stars of Heaven
 Calmly shone on earth below;
Goliad's men were sweetly sleeping,
 Never dreaming of the foe.

Wake not! stir not! Sleep on sweetly,
 Tho' an army's at the gate;
Hurrah, they charge, they rush upon you;
 Mexican, now meet thy fate!

Rousing from thy midnight slumbers,
 Rushing wildly, madly on,
" Yield thee, yield thee, to our brave ones,"
 Goliad's conquered ere the morn!

How the Texans' hearts glowed in them;
 How they felt this victory,
But a foretaste of the joys
 They would drink to Texas free!

'Twas in days of dark December,
  That our heroes southward came
To the walls of San Antonio, —
  San Antonio, sacred name!

Thus in ancient days 'twas christened
  By the dark-cowled Spanish priest,
Who to Anthony of Bees
  Yearly made a solemn feast.

Just beyond the city's shadow,
  In the morning cold and gray,
Lay the camps of Burleson,
  Ready for the bloody fray.

Some were fighting for their homes,
  For their wives, their children dear;
Things that always make men brave,
  Make them scorn the thought of fear!

But amid the troops of Texas
  Were a band of brothers brave,
Coming from the Crescent City,
  Just beyond the Gulf's blue wave.

They had left their homes behind them,
  Broken every kindred tie;
For the cause of liberty
  They had come to fight and die!

A uniform of gray they wore, —
    Prophetic of the days to be,
When all our Southern chivalry
    Should gather round the staff of Lee!

'Twas the morning of the fifth, —
    Fatal day to Mexico!
For 'twas then that Texas men
    Gained the Fort of Alamo.

In the town was heard, at dawning,
    Tramp of feet and voices' hum;
And adown the narrow streets
    See the dark-browed soldiers come!

Every loop-hole manned with men,
    Cannon blocking up the way;
Down those streets will blood be flowing
    Ere the closing of the day!

Hark! There comes the boom of cannon,
    Shake the walls of Alamo;
Oh! ye Texans, men of valor!
    Charge ye now upon the foe!

Up, Soledad, Acequia,
    Through Veramendi's walls of stone;
Through Garza's house there slowly comes
    Two bands of men, — two bands alone!

By Johnson and by Milam led,
 They slowly make, from day to day,
Amid the shot and booming shell,
 Unto the Alamo a way.

But ere they gain the costly stake,
 His brave heart pierced by rifle ball,
Great Milam, still at duty's post,
 A martyr to his creed doth fall.

The white flag waves from Alamo;
 What matters victory to him now?
When 'neath that flag he's lying low,
 The death dew on his noble brow!

The days of early spring have come;
 The prairie, touched with tints of green,
Invites the kiss of morning breeze;
 Along its slopes, in silver sheen,

The San Antonio's waters glide;
 With murmurs like the ocean shell,
That ever telleth of its home,
 It sings of springs amid the dell.

But soon, alas! its song of glee
 A tinge of deepest gloom will take,
And flowing down unto the sea,
 Its crystal tide red blood will flake;

The blood of Travis and his men,
　That staineth now and evermore
The history of the chieftain great
　Who reignèd then in Mexico.

For from the heights of Alazan
　The Mexic hosts are looking down ;
A cloud, whose rain shall be of blood,
　Is settling o'er the doomèd town !

Within the walls of Alamo,　　　　.
　A valiant band of helpless men,
Who vainly plead for help and aid
　Their little fortress to defend,

Are girding all their energy
　One desperate effort still to make,
And failing, then to bravely die,
　And seek the sleep whence none awake.

At midnight came the dreadful charge,
　With all the hideous sounds of strife ;
They pour upon our heroes few ;
　'Tis man for man, and life for life !

Each room becomes a battle-field,
　Made sacred by some hero's blood.
Oh ! God ! alas, defence is vain ;
　The foe comes onward like a flood !

At the cannon gallant Travis
  Bravely fought and bravely died;
E'en when dying, slew a foe
  With a sword-thrust in the side.

Bowie on his sick-bed lies,
  In a cell where monks have slept;
Cruel soldiers, bending o'er him,
  Have the ebbing life-blood sapped!

Crockett dies, his foes around him,
  Slaughtered by his trusty blade,
But his valor naught availeth,
  Santa Anna's lust will not be stayed!

Standing with the lighted match
  O'er the dreadful powder store,
Choosing rather thus to die,
  Evans falls; and many more —

Their names the Austin legend tells —
  Gave up their lives on that sad day;
Long lying buried where they fell,
  Mementoes of the boody fray.

Oh! Alamo, tho' fallen now,
  Thou art sacred in our eyes;
We sing an anthem unto thee,
  And shout it to the skies.

"Thou hadst thy couriers of defeat,
    Thermopylæ, thou glorious one;
More glorious still, in its sad fate,
    The Alamo had none!"

Think you that the chieftain's ire
    Was glutted by this bloody work?
Oh! no; he proved at Goliad
    A spirit worthy of the Turk!

It was on a night in March;
    Crowded in the Missions old
Were four hundred prisoned brothers,
    Each one cast in bravest mould.

Many from the hills of Georgia
    Came with Texas to unite;
'Mid those hills, so far away,
    Dear ones pray for them to-night, —

Pray that God may keep them safely,
    That their feet no more may roam!
Listen!   From the Mission walls
    Come the words of "home, sweet home!"

Little reck they that the morning
    Naught will bring but sorrow deep.
Oh! ye mothers, sisters, daughters,
    Far away in Georgia, weep!

13

Weep ye for the brave ones fallen,
　Not like men, with sword in hand,
But like common traitors shot,
　As in rank they guarded stand.

Oh! Santa Anna, murderer cruel,
　Think not that thine hour will last,
For a day of vengeance cometh, —
　Yes, that day is coming fast!

On the plains of San Jacinto,
　On the field with Houston brave,
Thou shalt bite the dust before him, —
　O'er thy camps his flag shall wave!

At the season when Queen Flora
　With her lovely flower train
Decks the prairies of the West,
　And bright blossoms fall like rain;

When the skies are bluer, fairer,
　And 'mid boughs the mock-birds dart,
Bringing with their strains of music
　The sweet spring-time of the heart, —

Such time it was; the April day
　Was fair and soft as Northern May,
While o'er the scene the day-king rose
　And shed his rays on friends and foes.

The San Jacinto's water clear
　Just rippled o'er the pebbles bright;
All looked as if that " Peace on Earth "
　Had fallen from the skirts of night.

Down-sloping to the river's bed,
　The plain looked fair unto the eye;
Beset with richest, rarest flowers,
　That near the water's side do lie.

The velvet leaves of Indian pink,
　Red cypress, with its waving plumes;
The dainty, dew-kissed primrose fair,
　The purple of wild clover blooms;

The fuschia wild, the daisy sweet,
　The Spanish dagger's thousand flowers,
That downward hang, like ivory bells
　Upon Titania's fairy towers.

On San Jacinto's honored plain
　The yellow sunlight's glory fell,
And bathed Santa Anna's Mexic camp
　And Houston's Texan men as well!

But with the red rays from the East
　There came the clamor and the din,
That follows in the wake of war,
　When men, by blood, sweet glories win.

All morn the stern-browed Texans went
    To and fro, from tent to tent,
And each one watched, with caution keen,
    What every stratagem might mean.

Brave men were there from many climes,
    They fought for but one common cause, —
To free themselves from Spanish rule,
    To live as men, 'neath freemen's laws!

They came from out their forest homes,
    And not a soul among them falters,
Brave planters from the Brazos Dios,
    And from the Colorado's waters.

Salado and San Marcos clear,
    And San Antonio's winding river,
Have sent the dwellers on their banks
    To make the Spaniards quake and quiver.

Because they lived in later days,
    Their praises yet unsung have been.
Are they less worthy of our lays
    Than Marion and his men?

They were a band of settlers brave;
    They fought against oppression dire.
Not all of Santa Anna's host
    Could smother freedom's burning fire!

'Tis afternoon, — siesta time ;
　　Within the camps of Mexico
All, all is silence and repose,
　　Except the tread, just to and fro,

Of half-wake sentinels, who guard
　　The rest of soldiers all round,
Who, wrapped in dreams of home perhaps,
　　On mother earth sleep fast and sound.

E'en Santa Anna, their great chief,
　　A man of blood, of wars, at best,
Who styled himself as Conqueror,
　　" The great Napoleon of the West," —

E'en he, upon his soldier's couch,
　　Is dreaming 'way the noontide hour.
Will his guardian angel send no sign
　　To warn him of the clouds that lower?

The eve was hot ; the warm south wind
　　Caressed the sleeper's hair and brow,
But whispered in his ear no tale
　　Of what the danger was, and how.

From out the thicket near the bank,
　　There came the pipe of the chaparral bird,
And the plover's restless, weird cry,
　　Far across the prairie was heard.

But suddenly out on the evening air
   The notes of the bugle rang sharp and clear,
And the vengeful tramp of soldiers' feet,
   Who came their life-long foes to meet.

The chieftain sprung from his bed with a start,
   And grasped his sword to his side ;
But many a comrade ne'er waked at all,
   For sleeping and dreaming they died !

Houston and his brave seven hundred
   Came rushing resistlessly on ;
The earth was trampled and dyed with blood,
   Where the flowers had bloomed at morn.

There's the rush, the roar of battle,
   The sword drinks the blood of the foe,
And 'bove the din is the battle-cry,
 "Remember the Alamo !"

The "Alamo" and "Goliad,"
   These were the magic words
That roused the fire in Texans' hearts
   And their souls to brave deeds stirred.

On to the carnage of death !
   On to the clasp of the foe !
On to the victory that waits thee !
 "Remember the Alamo !"

Routed and ruined, the Mexicans fall,
   Like flowers the reapers beneath;
Stricken with fear, they fly afar,
   And hide themselves on the heath.

The battle is over, the day is done;
   Victory comes with the setting sun,
Perches itself on that one "Lone Star."
   "Texas is free," they shout it afar!

Two score years and more have passed
   Since upon that April eve
Houston's men their laurels gained, —
   Laurels victory's crown to weave.

Where are now the men who stood
   On San Jacinto's plain that night,
In the fire-light of the camp,
   Talking o'er the hard-won fight?

Texas now, her "Lone Star" waving
   O'er her broad and fertile plains,
In herself a very kingdom,
   With her men of wit and brains,

Looketh on the glorious future,
   When her wealth shall trebled be;
When 'tis said, "There is none like her,
   Either on the land or sea."

In the grand old days of triumph
   Of the Grecian warriors bold,
Oft they sang in stirring story
   Of the tales their fathers told.

And as long as Grecian manhood
   To their heroes' deeds would turn,
In their pulses, quickly throbbing,
   Bravest, truest blood would burn.

But alas! when they, forgetting
   Noble acts of buried sires,
Sought to gain but wealth and pleasure,
   Then burned low their freedom's fires!

Then a race of slaves, becoming
   Brutalized by horrid crimes,
Naught was left of all their glory
   But their tales of other times.

This the fate that ever follows
   Nations who in ease forget
Deeds of men who, in Valhalla's
   Hall of Heroes now have met.

In our onward march to glory
   Let us not forget the past, —
All our riches quick may leave us;
   'Tis our history that will last!

Let us not forget those heroes,
    Warriors of our early times,
Whose brave deeds shall stand beside
    Events great in other climes.

Oh! ye men of Texas, never
    Stopping in your onward rush,
Power and wealth and fame to gain,
    While in manhood's early flush,

Pause one moment; let me show you
    One lone grave, unwatched, unkept;
See the railing falling rotten!
    O'er that tomb a nation wept!

See the wild flowers o'er it growing;
    They at least would deck his grave.
In the soft, sweet airs of summer,
    See the bending grasses wave!

Step you gently, now bend o'er it;
    Read the words engraven there!
'Tis the name of General Houston!
    He, whose every thought and care

Was for Texas, for her glory.
    Oh! what shame there is upon her,
That her hero, lying lowly,
    Hath no soul his dust to honor!

Kneeling by the hero's side,
   Thus I lift mine eyes and pray,
" God of Battles, God of Justice,
   Hear, oh hear, my humble lay;

" Rouse the fire in Texans' hearts,
   Fitting monument to raise,
That a shaft of Parian marble,
   Rising fair in future days,

" O'er the sacred dust of Houston,
   Shall his deeds of valor show,
That our land may not forget him,
   As in death he lieth low ! "

JANUARY 1, 1879.

While the earth was wrapped in silence,
While the winds were wild and drear,
There were tears last night, and sadness,
O'er the bed of the dying year.
When at noon the sun above us
Looked down for the last, last time,
On the year that was to leave us
At the ringing of midnight chime,
He seemed half sad, at the parting
With his friend, for the months gone by,
And sank, with a face mist-veilèd,
To his home in the western sky.
When the twilight fell at even
Over the earth so cold,
And into its mystical shadows
The throbbing world enrolled,
The night-wind, rushing by us,

Sobbed like a grief-struck heart,
And seemed to whisper sadly,
" Old year, we soon must part."
From the tiny clock on the mantel
The hours rang sad, tho' clear ;
They seemed to know they were telling
The death of the dear Old Year.
Nine, from the clock on the mantel ;
Ten, from the high church-tower ;
Eleven, — how the minutes are flying ;
There's only another hour ;
Then in the silent night,
Glorious in its gloom,
The spirits twelve, in sadness, lay
The " Old Year " in his tomb.
He has grown weak and weary,
In his journey of twelve months' time ;
Over his breast is falling
His beard, like snowy rime.
Closed are his eyes forever ;
Folded the weary hands,
Like the useless sails of a craft
Becalmed near Southern strands.
He is dead !   He is gone forever !
In the tomb of the buried years
He lies in stately grandeur,

Unmoved by smiles or tears.
Wreathed in his locks of silver,
He wears, in a kingly crown,
Twelve jewels of hues resplendent, —
Twelve jewels of great renown.
He is dead!   No more will we greet him, —
Tho' to many a heart he was dear,
For lips now silent forever
Had called him a " Happy New Year!"
He is dead!   And what has he left us?
What thoughts for the New Year bright?
Open the will and read it, —
Read it, I pray you, aright.
A happy year it was to some,
A year of joy and mirth;
Perhaps another like it, ne'er
Will come to them on earth.
To some, 'twas half made up of smiles,
And half made up of tears;
'Twas freighted oft with happiness,
'Twas often filled with fears.
But other souls there are, oh God!
To whom this year has brought
Unbounded sadness, death and gloom,
In plague-struck cities wrought.
Beside that river grand, that flows

With yellow surges down,
By cities lovely as a dream,
By many a stately town;
Until, at last, unwearièd,
Its deep red surges free,
Rush with a mighty grandeur
And rest within the sea !
Throughout the lovely valley
Where its mighty waters sweep,
The pall of Death has fallen
In shadows long and deep.
Like to a mighty giant,
There came to this land so fair,
A demon, in robes of saffron, —
A demon, from out his lair !
He came to the crowded city,
He crouched in the green-woods shade,
And daily upon the altar
His quivering victims laid.
Long did the shadows enfold them;
All hope for the future seemed gone;
Their wails were the vespers at even;
Their tears, as the dew-drops at morn.
'Till unto the stricken people
There came, like an angel of light,
A spirit, whose power was stronger, —

He came, like a ghost, in the night.
In his hand, that was cold and icy,
He carried a glittering spear;
He struck at the heart of the demon,
Who, shuddering, died in fear.
Then he chained him in bands of ice,
And wrapt him in robes of snow;
And calmed were the people's wailing;
And hushed were the sounds of woe.
To them, in their desolation,
When the New Year's tide comes in,
And they think of the voices silent,
And the forms, that never again
Shall gather around the fireside
When the leaves are dry and sere, —
To them, of thy stricken fold, oh God!
It has been a sad Old Year!
It has been a year of harvest rich
Throughout our broad, fair land;
In all the barns, on all the farms
The smiling sheaves do stand.
Across the fields of waving grain
The Autumn sunshine fell,
Upon the ears of golden corn,
And ripened them full well;
Upon the wheat, that bending down

Their heads of bearded grain,
Had grown to be thus good and fair
Thro' Summer sun and rain;
And every fruit that mother earth
Doth yield to sons of men,
From North and South and East and West,
Have yielded twice again.
A peace-crowned year; fit offering
To Him whose love's divine;
Oh! grant that round our other years
Sweet Peace shall always shine!
And now there comes the glad New Year,
In youthful vigor proud, —
List to the sounds of mirth and joy
That rise from every crowd.
" Hail to the New Year joyous,
That reigns o'er all the earth!
Oh! welcome him all people,
With hearts of joy and mirth!
Right royally he wears his crown,
Right bravely sits his throne,
And looks, with kindling eye, upon
The kingdom, all his own."

THE ORIGIN OF THE MOSS-ROSE.

"It is spring!   The Queen is here!
　　Ye loyal hearts, awake, awake!
And chant aloud your hymns of praise,
　　For fair Queen Flora's sake."
These were the South Wind's gentle words,
　　Through all the spring-time hours,
As, bending o'er the sleeping ones,
　　He kissed them into flowers.

In Queen Flora's fair dominion,
　　Loyal hearts are there, and true;
Each one listened to the summons,
　　Told it to the morning dew, —
How the dew-drops glinted, glistened,
　　Fairly dancing in their glee,
For they longed to deck the flowers
　　With their sparkling jewelry.

E'en the robins in the tree-tops,
　　And the lark, that wings his flight
14

Through the realms of ether blue,
  To the morn's fair land of light,
Heard the message to the flowers, —
  Heard it, too, with hearts of glee, —
And their songs were all the sweeter,
  And their flight was still more free.

All the land was bright with promise
  Of the beauties yet to be;
All the earth was filled with gladness
  At the birds' sweet minstrelsy.
In a garden where the flowrets
  Spring like fairies from the earth;
Where all lovely buds and blossoms
  Have their being and their birth,

Dwelt the Queen of all the flowers,
  With her loyal subjects round her;
Not a one in her dominion
  Would by word or action wound her.
Oh! her train of lords and ladies,
  They were very fair to view!
In their robes of hues so brilliant,
  And their ornaments of dew.

'Twas one morning in the May-time,
  When the floral world was gay
With her wealth of varied colors, —
  Tints that mock the dawn of day!

All adown the lovely garden,
   Ran a whisper 'mong the flowers, —
Such a fluttering ne'er was heard,
   Such a stir, for hours and hours!

Would you like to know the secret
   That the flowers told each other?
"Ah," they said, "it must be true,
   For it comes from our Queen Mother!"
On the day that dawns to-morrow,
   It will be the first of June,
While the summer birds are piping
   To the world a merry tune,

There's to be a flower wedding!
   Not that such a thing is strange
Is this chattering and fluttering
   Up and down the flower range,
For amid Queen Flora's subjects
   Marriages have oft occurred;
'Tis the *difference* in their stations
   That this noise among them stirred.

That the fair and dainty Rose,
   All arrayed in robes of white,
Gleaming, from her bower of emeralds,
   Like a snowy water-sprite,
Should so stoop to those beneath her,
   As to wed with one so low

As the Brown Moss, rough and shaggy, —
Such a thing was strange, I trow!

She had been a maid of honor
    In the gay court of the Queen;
Many a gallant, gay lord-lover,
    All bedecked in silver sheen,
Had beside her softly lingered,
    Sought in vain for her fair hand;
But to wed her own true lover,
    Tho' the lowest in the land,

She hath passed the lordlings by,
    Bid them seek some other shrine,
Whose fair priestess fain would listen
    To their words and phrases fine.
She will wed upon the morrow
    With her lover, tried and true;
In his homely coat of brown
    He hath won the praise of few;

But a heart that's good and noble
    Is a jewel all should prize, —
And the White Rose found the jewel,
    Tho' 'twas hid by rough disguise.
All her young life he has loved her,
    Watched her with a jealous eye,
Smiled whene'er she looked upon him;
    Now when summer days are nigh,

When there comes the month of roses,
    Comes the "merry month of June,"
With its odors and its perfumes,
    And its choristers in tune,
He will claim her as his own,
    Guard her life against all woes,
Clasp her, kiss her like a lover, —
    His fair bride, the snowy Rose!

How the flowers chattered, whispered,
    As the invitations sent
By the hand of Morning Zephyr,
    To the high and lowly went.
Thus a tall and queenly lily,
    To a flaunting Dahlia said,
"How can White Rose wed so lowly?
    I would rather far be dead!"

Proudly spoke a rare Geranium,
    As it shook its scarlet blooms,
To the Heliotrope, its neighbor,
    Rich in sweetest of perfumes,
"This is sure the oddest marriage, —
    Such a lord I would not own;
I would rather live forever
    All forgo'ten and alone."

Thus her sweetly-scented neighbor
    To the proud Geranium spoke,

And her voice, as clear it sounded,
    Some " Forget-me-nots " awoke :
" She has shown the poorest taste, —
    But pray let her have her way ;
She is spoiled and so conceited
    That no one can say her nay."

Then a Fuschia joined the confab,
    While she smoothed her waxen bells,
From whose hearts the truant wild-bee
    Gathers honey for his cells,—
" She will have *one* consolation, —
    Jealousy she'll never feel,
For no other flower will ever
    His affections try to steal."

Sneered the Yellow Rose, near by her,
    At the Fuschia's laughing speech,
Like those envious ones who hate
    Every thing they cannot reach, —
" I am sure *she* is no beauty ;
    She is doing well, *I* think,
Her pale face and poorer fortune
    To the Brown Moss thus to link."

Then up spoke the noble Calla :
    " Shame upon you, sisters mine,
Thus to speak of one so pure,
    True and loveliest of her kind.

Only marry where you love,
　　Is the maxim of the flowers;
If for gold, like mortals, wedding,
　　Soon we'd lose our fairy powers.

" Where the White Rose's love is given,
　　There, there only will it rest;
She will yield her lord true homage,
　　Tho' in Brown Moss he is dressed."
Thus the flowers in the garden,
　　Spoke their thoughts about the pair,
Some there were who'd not believe it;
　　Some there were who did not care.

But the Lilies of the Valley,
　　Stirring all their waxen cups,
Filled with nectar for Titania,
　　When with them at eve she sups;
And the graceful bending ferns,
　　Feathers from the fairies' wings,
'Mid whose leaves the elfins nestle,
　　Emblems of all dainty things,

Joined the Pansies, golden-hearted,
　　In a song to him above,
As they whispered to each other, —
　　" The sweetest of thy gifts is *love*."
To their song the White Rose listened, —
　　Listened while her quivering heart,

Rosy-tinted with emotion,
   Told the story of love's dart.

'Tis the day! the wedding day!
   The flowers are wakened at morn
By the kiss of the loving sunshine
   And the sound of the zephyr's horn,
As loud and clear he winds it,
   And flies o'er hill and dale,
To bring the wedding summons
   To all within the vale.

Within the Queen's fair palace,
   Will be the wedding grand,
And never a wedding like it,
   Was seen in all the land.
And every bud and blossom,
   And every flower was there,
All dressed in gayest garments,
   To view the happy pair.

Geraniums, Roses, Lilies,
   The Dahlias, tall and gay.
And e'en that dainty flowret,
   The poet's "eye of day;"
And the naiad-like "Lily of the Vale," —
   "My thoughts are white," she saith, —
And the starry Jasmine of Charity,
   And the Ivy leaf of Faith.

From out the gayly surging crowd
   The purple Violets peep, —
The emblems of humility,
   Of love so true and deep;
And the fragrant blooms of Mignonette,
   And the wild flowers from the bank,
And the dark green moss that springs
   Where the weeds grow deep and dank.

All these, and many more I ween,
   To the flower-wedding came,
But each and all in their beauty fair,
   I find 'tis hard to name.
The birds all twittered together,
   " What shall the music be?"
The Robin will sing a solo
   From the top of his favorite tree.

There will be the grandest chorus,
   From the forest minstrels sweet ; —
The Lark shall sing soprano,
   The Mock-bird tenor sweet;
The Blue-bird's steady alto,
   And the deep notes of the Thrush,
Will make a song so lovely
   That all the world will hush.

The bells of the Morning Glories
   Shall ring the wedding chimes,

With musical, heavenly measure,
  Like the closing of sweetest rhymes.
But hush, the bridal train has come;
  The wedding-march sounds loud,
As close beside her chosen one,
  The White Rose walketh proud.

Before the throne where Flora sits,
  They lowly bend the knee,
The groom in his homely coat of brown,
  And the bride — she was fair to see!
So hushed in silence was the crowd
  That not a whisper fell
Upon the air that summer morn,
  Till rang the wedding bell.

The lovely Queen her blessing gave,
  While happiness untold
The zephyrs and the sunshine wished
  Each day would sweet unfold.
From all the birds in all the trees
  Broke forth a chorus grand,
And the echoes of their songs were heard
  Thro' all the summer land.

And proudly did the Brown Moss look
  Upon his pure young bride,
As in her snowy robes she stood,
  His own — whate'er betide!

A robe, all made of dainty moss,
　He round her gleaming shoulders threw, —
And lo ! as o'er her form it fell,
　She gained a beauty new.

And ever since that bridal day
　In Flora's wide domain,
All other flowers quick have paled
　And felt their beauty wane
Before the Moss Rose, twice as fair,
　Since close around her form
She wears the cloak her lover gave,
　To shield her from the storm !

IN MEMORIAM.

WRITTEN IN MEMORY OF WM. F. GORDON, WHO DIED
NEAR FORT CONCHO, TEXAS, DEC. 29, 1879.

Far, far from home, no touch of loving kindred;
  No mother's kiss to soothe the pangs of death;
No woman's hand to press the brow, dew-dampened;
  No woman's ear to catch his latest breath.

Oh! mothers, mothers, who have lost your chil-
    dren, —
  Have seen them sink before your weeping eyes,
Think on the grief of her whose child is absent,
  With not one home-voice near him when he dies!

'Twas thus he lay; the dreary winds of winter
  Rushed o'er the prairies of the lonely land.
Beside him stood his comrades strong yet tender, —
  But whose could soothe him like a mother's hand!

And so he died; and o'er his grave will murmur
  The tender grasses in the days of spring;
Mayhap a wild flower, sweet with breath of summer,
  Its bloom and fragrance to the spot will bring.

At night the fire-flies, ever lightly swinging
  Their fairy lamps amid the dusk and dew,
Will guard his rest; 'tis meet that things of nature
  Should watch the grave of one so good and true!

And there at eve the restless, wearied plover,
  With shrill, wild cry will call unto its mate;
And there the dove, with sweet, low voice complaining,
  Will moan her song o'er his untimely fate.

He sleeps in death! Beyond the hours of waking, —
  Dear, faithful friend! Toll slow the funeral bell!
Beyond all ties of making and of breaking,
  Our friend sleeps sweet and well.

Beyond all days of acting and of dreaming;
  Beyond all hours of happiness or woe;
Beyond the real and beyond the seeming;
  Beyond the tides that slowly come and go;

Far, far beyond their ebbing and their flowing;
  Beyond the rise and setting of the sun;
Beyond the coming and beyond the going;
  In peace of heaven, our dead and dear loved one!

Beyond the blooming and beyond the fading
 Of bud and flower, of tender leaf and tree ;
Beyond the shining and beyond the shading,
 He rests, he rests in deep eternity.

No more for him the smiling and the weeping, —
 His smiles, his tears are done ;
For him no more the sowing and the reaping, —
 His prize, his crown is won.

Beyond our touch, beyond our sight forever;
 Beyond the gifts that loving hands have wrought ;
Beyond all power we have to bind or sever, —
 But not, thank God ! oh ! not beyond our thought !

A NEW YEAR'S HYMN.

Hail to the New Year! Thus the joyous crowd
   Have sung from age to age;
Thus, long ago, with mirth and laughter loud,
   The beardless youth and snowy-headed sage
Sang 'midst the streets of Rome;
The Tiber's red and yellow turgid foam
Caught up the sound; and from its banks,
   The echoes came again: —
" Hail to the New Year! Happy day, All Hail!
   Be free, most free from every thought of pain!
And we of later days are ringing still
   The joyous bells, when comes the New Year in
With robes as white as snow-drop, sweet and pale,
   All spotless yet from taint and soil of sin.
Come near! Come near! Thou new-born child of
     Time !
   That standest pure, with red lips undefiled, —

With eyes undimmed and brow unfurrowed yet;
  What dost thou here, where winds blow strong and
    wild ?
But see, he smiles ! His bright curls backward thrown,
  As some young Prince, he laughs the winds to
    scorn !
Thou knowest thy power, thou knowest the year is
    thine, —
  Thy rule began ere came the hour of morn !
Thine now the power to rule the hours and days,
  And thine the power to bring us joy and grief;
Thou reignest now o'er kingdoms, cities, men, —
  Within thy hand lies fate of flower and leaf;
'Tis thine to touch the dainty, dreamy buds,
  And usher them to fragrant life and bloom.
Within our hearts are holy flowers of faith;
  Like earthly flowers they sprang from out the
    gloom;
Touch thou their petals with thy magic hand,
  That they may blossom in the light of Heaven,
And comfort us, when, wearied of the day,
  We rest and dream beside the hearth at even !
Tis thine to bring to sweet perfection's taste,
  The purpling cluster of the graceful vine, —
The downy peach with crimson mantling cheek, —
  The clear-skinned plum and dusky muscadine.

And thine the touch that ripens into gold
   The ears of corn, in many a fertile field,
And bearded wheat upon the upland plain,
   And every grain that gives to man its yield.
Hail to the New Year! Hope of hopeful hearts,
   Who standing in thy light, all eagerly,
With strainèd eyes and crimson lips apart,
   Watch for their ships, far, far across the sea, —
The white-winged ships, whose coming they have
      waited
   Thro' days of spring, and sleepy summer days;
Thro' days when autumn's sunshine gaily tinted
   The forest leaves in all the upland ways;
Thro' winter days, with icy breath o'erladen,
   When angered waves dashed o'er the dreary sands,
They watched the coming from some distant Aiden,
   The ships that tarried in the tropic lands.
But in thy light the darkening shadows flee!
All doubts, all fears, sink in the secret sea!
The days of waiting, when the ships came not,
Grow dim in memory, and are soon forgot.
And wilt thou bring the joys for which we hunger?
   And wilt thou bring the friends of other years?
New Year! Without them we will often weary, —
   Bring back those days, but not their meed of tears!
Bright day of hope, our every grief and sorrow

Within the depths of last year's grave we cast;
All anger, hate, and jealous demons harbored,
   Are laid to rest within the shadowed past.
Then give us Hope to paint a glowing picture,
   More bright in hues than canvas of Lorraine;
And Happiness for our most royal sovereign,
   And all thy days for his joy-laden reign.
If thou wilt give us such a loving artist,
   If thou wilt give us such a lordly King,
We'll sing thy praise, oh, New Year, bright and joy-
      ous, —
   Hark! on the air the merry greetings ring!

SUFFERING ERIN.

READ FOR THE BENEFIT OF IRISH SUFFERERS, AT THE
OPERA HOUSE, WACO, TEXAS, FEBRUARY 19, 1880.

Oh! Saint of Erin, come thou near to-night,
  And touch my tongue with burning fire intense,
That I may tell thy woes unutterable,
  With heartfelt passion and strong eloquence.
Oh! dreams of beauty, that are woven round
  Thy magic name, thou green-clad, beauteous isle,
Come near and soothe my senses with sweet sound,
  And let me linger in thy charm awhile!

Oh! could I watch by fair Killarney's lake,
  And weave, in verse, the beauties of that scene,
Or pluck the heather from the heights of Bloom,
  Or feast mine eyes upon thy valleys green;
Could I but linger 'mid thy castles old, —
  Explore the turret, mount the ruined stair,
Moss-grown and rugged; list the weird tales
  Of kings who erst had made their dwellings there.

Could I but listen to those Shandon bells, —
    Those sweet-toned bells beside the " river Lee," —
Sweet land of Erin!   If such fate were mine,
    Then would I dare to sing a song for thee! —
A song for thee, thou sea-locked child of ocean,
    Engirt on every side by shining sands;
Thy children yield thee truest heart devotion,
    Tho' wandering far amid the foreign lands.

Still, still they turn, with patriotic fervor,
    To dreams of thee, tho' far in Western wild;
Not years of change can break the chain that bindeth
    The land of Erin to her wandering child.
Still, still, they dream that soon the sweet time cometh,
    When Ireland, from lowly bended knee,
Shall raise herself to heights of ancient grandeur,
    And rule again, proud island of the sea!

If such their love, when naught of danger threatens,
    What must it be when sufferings line her brow, —
When sorrowing, her children all ahungered,
    She standeth sad, as e'en she standeth now?
And need I ask what generous meed they gave her,
    What faithful love is theirs, in hours like this?
The Irish heart is warm, and warmer even
    In days of sadness than in days of bliss!

'Tis like the harp, whose rich chords deeply answer
    A tender touch with tender melody;

And sorrowful it giveth back the music,
  Whene'er we touch upon the sorrow key.
Around us Ireland's hearts to-day are bleeding;
  Around us Irish hands are sending out
Their generous gifts; her cause needs not our pleading;
  In suffering's hour we must not pause or doubt!

From Coleraine, upon the banks of Bann,
  From Errigal, the mountain by the sea,
To where the Suir, Bana, and Barrow pour
  Their waters down like some sweet psaltery;
Beside the Erne, whence Shannon's waters flow
  'Twixt curving banks, by many a rocky nook,
Where wild arbutus flings its trailing hair,
  Close by the purling of some mountain brook;

By Liffey's stream, from Curragh of Kildare,
  From famed Killarney's winding chain of lakes
That lie, like necklace made of jewels rare,
  In sheets of sapphire hue — a cry awakes!
A wail of anguish from the sorrowing ones, —
  A wail that echoes through her winding dells,
And travels fast beside the ocean's roar,
  Till on our shore its piteous tale it tells.

List! Can ye hear it? Silence, silence all!
  Hold fast your breath! It is a sound of dread!
Can you not hear the voice of strong men wailing,
  And little children crying " Bread, bread!"

Across the Atlantic's breast of foam it comes,
    Within the train of winter's stinging blast,
And brings such thoughts of Erin's grief and woe
    As chill our blood, and leave us all aghast.

Can ye not see them?   Look! those faces pale;
    The brows where Famine sits, so gaunt and wild;
The hollow eyes, so sunk, yet burning still
    With wolfish gleams of Fever — Famine's child!
The shrunken limbs, the voice so weak and faint,
    The anguished lips, the lowly bended head;
And evermore the wailing children's call;
    And evermore the women's cry for bread!

Can you not hear them weeping, weeping, weeping,
    Can you not hear them crying to their God?
Can you not see the rude, rough pauper's coffin,
    Can you not hear the dismal falling sod?
With dreary, weird, awful sound it falleth;
    With sharp, hard thud, as tho' it were a stone;
The hollow-eyed and gaunt-limbed mourners standing
    Beside the grave, too weak for tears or moan.

A picture rises, clearly cut, before me:
    A homely cabin by the lonely sea,
Where greenish waves come darkling to the shore,
    And winter winds moan low and piteously.
Within the hut are crouched God's creatures five —
    And they are starving, starving! oh, my brothers!

The little ones are crying in the night-time, —
   But all in vain; the weary-hearted mothers

Hush them to rest. The dreams of sleep come not,
   For ever gnaws that sharpened hunger pain !
And mother songs are turned to prayers for food,
   And " give us bread " is still its sad refrain !
With pinched, wild faces, see them bending o'er
   The peat fire burning dimly thro' the gloom ;
The wailing winds creep thro' each yawning crevice,
   And sound a death-march thro' the darkened room.

A fitful gleam leaps from the fire a moment,
   And lights the scene, — as when near hour of death,
The weary spirit for a moment seemeth
   Strong as of yore, then sinks with dying breath ;
A moment's brightness and the darkness falls ; —
   I see no more, a mist doth vail mine eyes !
But still I hear that deep wail — " Give us bread ! "
   And still I hear the sad young children's cries.

www.ingramcontent.com/pod-product-compliance
Lightning Source LLC
Chambersburg PA
CBHW020110030726
47498CB00006B/2044